Becoming Vincent

The Wild Ones #1

C.M. Owens

Becoming A Vincent
The Wild Ones #1
Copyright © 2017 by C.M. Owens

When you live in a place where "turbo speed" internet is a slight step above dial-up, men carry on nine-year beard-growing challenges out of stubborn pride, and your brothers do things like nail all your shoes to the floor of your cabin just for funsies, you tend to be a little crazy. You can call it a locational hazard, if you will.

That's Tomahawk for you.

We rank people based on just how crazy you are. And the four craziest families in town are called the Wild Ones.

I'm on the bottom tier of those, so technically I'm not *as* crazy as the other Wild Ones. In fact, if it wasn't for my brothers and their endless antics, I wouldn't be considered a Wild One at all. Ahem. Sure. We'll go with that.

Anyway, I have a best friend who endures it all with me. Benson Nolans is my one constant favorite person.

Without him, I'd probably go really crazy, and not the fun kind. It'd be ridiculous, after three years of a flawless friendship, to mess that all up by falling for him.

I mean, even if we did get a little too close one night, it'd be reckless endangerment. Even if we did suddenly feel the chemistry that's always been there and stop toeing the line, it'd be a foolish risk to take.

It'd be stupid to start hoping a really fun, but completely irrational, night with zero inhibitions might accidentally happen.

Really stupid...

Right?

Chapter 1

Wild Ones Tip #189
You only have two legs.
Animals with sharp claws and teeth have four.
Never get caught in the woods without your gun.

LILAH

"You big bastard! Get away from the tree, and no one has to die," I shout at the hostile cougar that is debating whether or not she wants to climb up after me.

I even wiggle a puny stick at her like it's Excalibur or something.

How did I end up in a tree, wielding a stick like a mythical sword, while a cougar decides if I'm worth the trouble of mauling to death or not? Two reasons: Hale and Killian Vincent.

Those are my brothers.

I'm one third of a set of fraternal triplets. My theory is that all the oxygen in the womb was cut off from the two jackasses who are responsible for my current predicament, and I'm the only one who escaped with functioning brain cells.

Sometimes they act like geniuses, other times…they leave me in the woods with a freaking cougar! And not the kind of cougar who has a hankering for a younger guy. Nope. I'd like that cougar.

I'm talking about a cougar with sharp claws, sharper teeth, and a lot of power that could destroy me.

1

The cougar groans or growls or both. I'm not really sure.

I don't speak cougar, but I think that was a sound of frustration, and fortunately, she decides not to shimmy up the tree after me.

I blow out a breath of relief as the cougar slinks off into the thick woods, a kitten cougar joining her at her side, and they slowly disappear from sight. Obviously I don't get in any sort of hurry to climb down, just in case that momma cougar is tricky and is playing me.

Fun fact: most animals are faster than humans. Much faster. Like, you can't possibly outrun most four-legged creatures no matter what the movies try to tell you.

Shotguns sound in the distance, and I glare in their direction.

Those assholes are going to end up with me shooting them with buckshot in the asses. Again.

This time it will be on purpose.

Slowly, warily, and all too shakily, I start the treacherous climb down, stepping on a few questionable branches that creak and quiver as I do.

More shotgun blasts continue, at least staying in the opposite direction of my cougar stalker so that I don't have to worry about it being driven right back at me.

As soon as my feet hit the ground, I sprint. In my head, I'm an Olympic runner right now, and nothing can catch me as I put on a gold medal performance.

My heartbeat thumps in my ears as I run harder and faster than I ever have, leaping over fallen trees or bushes like they're intentional hurdles. And I run for a solid mile or more, right to my aunt's cabin where people are everywhere.

I collapse as soon as I'm surrounded by gun-wielding, bearded men.

"Lilah! Why are you so sweaty?"

I'm wheezing for air, barely able to lift an arm to signal that I'm alive, haphazardly sprawled on the ground, and my aunt is furiously inquiring about my sweatiness.

Awesome.

"You okay?" I hear someone ask.

Benson. That's Benson. I think. My ears are still letting me hear too much of my heartbeat too loudly to be sure. Please let it be Benson. He'll save me.

Surely he'll realize the after-running effects are slowly killing me, and he'll have to save me.

Oxygen. I need a lot of it.

"Lilah?" the guy asks again, but I just wheeze out an unintelligible sound, struggling to catch a breath.

Despite what my mind thought during that muscle-burning sprint for my life, I'm not actually an Olympic runner. I'm a run-to-survive-only kind of girl. I'm always suspicious of those people who say they run for fun.

Personally, if you're running regularly, I assume you're hiding something nefarious and practicing your getaway for whatever is coming after you. And I don't want to be your friend, because I hate running.

Someone scoops me up, and my eyes roll around lazily, taking in the bearded face of my lifter.

Benson. I knew it.

I groan a sound that is supposed to be appreciation, and he cradles me closer.

More gunshots from farther out have me narrowing my eyes again.

"What are those jackass brothers of yours shooting at when we're having a party?" my aunt demands.

Words still aren't working out so well for me, so I just continue to stare and wheeze.

Did I mention I hate running?

They're shooting to "guide" me out of the woods, as though I don't know which direction to go. Pricks.

The gunshots grow silent, while Benson continues to hold me. His beard is annoying me at the moment, causing me to fidget. Really, who needs a beard that long? It's tickling my stomach on the sliver of skin that is   showing where my shirt has risen up.

I hate beards. And I'm constantly surrounded by them.

"Lilah, I'm going to ask you one more time—"

"Cougar," I manage to say, interrupting my aunt.

Her eyes grow wide.

"Kai Wilder's cougar?" she asks, unconcerned.

"Ha! No. Wild momma cougar," I say, my pants growing shallower as my breaths come easier.

"You sure?" she asks, putting her hands on her hips.

"Pretty fucking sure, but I didn't hang out to check her belly for a scar, since she was trying to kill me or whatever."

Benson snorts, and my aunt turns about ten shades of red.

"Go get cleaned up. Use the soap on your mouth. Your date is coming to meet you in…well, shit. He should already be here."

My date. How did I forget the date?

My aunt has been trying to marry me off since I turned eighteen. That was six years ago.

She's old school. I'm surprised she waited until I was eighteen, if I'm being honest.

If it'd been up to her, and if I had been more mature — *pfft* — I'd have been married by sixteen and popping out babies by eighteen, like my mother. But it wasn't up to her. Still isn't. And I'm still not mature enough for tiny human making.

Women cook. Men bring home the bacon. Yada yada yada. Her mind is set in stone on how things should work.

I'm self-sufficient as far as finances go, so no thank you to the husband's paycheck.

"Right," I say, knowing appeasing her is easier than arguing with her.

Benson lowers me to my feet, making sure I'm steady before he releases me, and I thank him, patting him on the chest and ignoring his beard that tickles my hand.

I head in, wash up, check to make sure I'm not a solid shade of red from all that exertion, and reemerge just in time to see…Mr. Fucking Gorgeous.

Yep.

The guy is so pretty that my eyes hurt.

Wow.

Where the hell did she find him? Not that I want to date him. The guy is too pretty to be anything less than suspicious, but still…

"Oh! Lilah, this is Liam. Liam, my niece — Lilah."

Liam. Nope. Two L names would just cause confusion.

I still drink in the sight of him, because Liam is pretty, and I like looking at him. It's been a while since I saw someone past puberty without a beard.

He thrusts his hand out, and I note it's tan and a little calloused, meaning he possibly spends time outside and working with his hands. Or he jacks off outside a lot. One of the two.

His blond hair looks incredibly touchable. His smooth jaw is definitely a refreshing sight next to all the overgrown beards in this place.

This *place* being Tomahawk, Washington, a small lake community in the middle of no-damn-where, and a hop, skip and jump away from the Canadian border...which is also right in the middle of no-damn-where.

I'm always leery of newcomers, because...back to that running thing.

If you didn't grow up in Tomahawk, then the only reason you'd be here is to run from something somewhere else.

"Nice to meet you," I say, smiling.

His grin is immediate, but I can tell he's no more interested in me than I am in him. He looks distracted, if I'm being honest. In fact, I think he's searching for someone as he looks around.

My poor aunt is going to have to wait on all those babies she wants me to pop out. She probably dragged him out here.

"What brings you to Tomahawk?" I ask conversationally.

Population? Three hundred.

"Just moved here."

Correction, three hundred and one.

"Why?" I ask reflexively.

"Lilah!" my aunt scolds.

"It's a reasonable question. Ninety-five percent of the country doesn't even know we exist. The other five percent like to pretend we don't."

Liam laughs under his breath, glancing down at his feet for a minute. "Long story. Your aunt tells me you do some online graphic designing."

I just nod, deciding not to go down that boring road of what we each do for a living.

"Have a seat, Liam. Lilah, you sit next to him," my aunt says without an ounce of subtlety

"It's less painful if you just roll with it and let her think she's winning."

"I can hear you," Aunt Penny grumbles.

Liam's grin only grows as I say, "I know. We can hear you too."

Per the usual, I take a seat by Benson on the forever long picnic table, and he elbows me gently. "What about that cougar?" he asks as Liam sits down on my other side.

"Cougar?" Liam asks, intrigued.

I shrug, not looking at either of them as we start passing plates around. The food is in the center of the table, and you scoop something out of the bowl in front of you and pass it to the next person.

Liam catches onto this pretty quickly, even though it's his first time.

"Big momma cougar with a nasty temper," I finally say.

Cougars aren't that uncommon around here, but it's rare they chase you down...unless there's a damn cub involved.

"What were you doing out in the woods without a gun?" Benson asks, a little bit of an edge to his tone.

I cast him a sidelong glance, but he's practically glaring at me. All you can see on his face are his eyes, most of his nose and a little of his forehead, because…black beard. A lot of black beard.

"I was in the woods with my brothers, who both had a gun."

"Brothers?" Liam asks, and Benson grunts like he's irritated with the interruption.

I face Pretty Boy. "I have two brothers. We're Triplets. I'm the only one who survived the womb with a sense of self-preservation and common sense. Or maybe it's because I was the only one of the three who was blessed with a vagina."

To this, the entire table laughs, except for my aunt, who is groaning and covering her face, shaking her head as though she's embarrassed.

"Are they here?" Liam asks so innocently, bypassing the whole vagina remark.

Idly, I wonder if he's embarrassed to talk about the female anatomy, and grin to myself, filing away that information for future use.

When no one answers him, he asks the question again. "Seriously, are they here?" He looks around the table like he's searching them out.

More laughter ensues, but not from Aunt Penny. "Those heathens aren't allowed over here anymore when I entertain," she tells him, passing a plate along. "Not for a long while. Hopefully they'll grow up."

Aunt Penny will lift the ban soon. She always does. My brothers will be back over here in no time and she knows it. She can't help herself, because she loves them.

I scoop out more of the yams and pass the plate along to Liam.

"We went into the woods looking for the right tree. Those jerks broke my bed—"

"Broke your bed?" Liam interrupts, arching an eyebrow.

I really don't like what he's insinuating, but since he's doing it with a playful smirk that I can see because there's no beard on his pretty face, I let it pass.

"They were standing on my bed to try and steal my ceiling fan after they broke theirs. Our cabins are side by side. They break in. All the time. No boundaries, those two. So, the bed broke under their combined weight, and I planned to make them build me a new one with a tree or two of my choosing."

He blinks at me. But Benson is the one to chuckle, drawing my attention back to him.

"Your bed wasn't strong enough to support two people?" the bearded man asks me, eyes twinkling with humor.

I narrow my eyes on him. "Do you think any guy would make it to the bedroom with *my* brothers next door?"

He cocks his head like he's thinking about it. "Good point," he concedes.

"I have to travel when I want to get mine."

The humor leaves his eyes, and I grin while tugging his beard a little. He grunts, and I turn back to see Liam smiling broadly at me. Oh, yeah. I probably shouldn't be talking so openly in front of him.

Plates finally stop being passed, and I start eating mine, leaning a little on Benson since I don't know Liam and don't like brushing up against strangers over and over. Plus, I'm really tired. And Benson never minds being leaned on.

Liam's eyes flick between us, probably getting the wrong idea, but I don't really care. I have no desire to pop out little Liam babies.

He glances around at all the beards — literally. Then he reaches up and touches the side of his baby smooth face. I'll be honest, I am tempted to do that too. I can't remember the last time I saw a smooth face on a full grown man.

Well, I can. Three years ago, which was the last time I had sex. The guy was passing through, and I decided to pass through his cabin rental. He didn't mind. It was a really great night.

Sigh.

If I had known it'd be three years' worth of drought after that, it would have been even more fun.

"So, how'd you end up with the cougar if your brothers were out there?" Benson asks, even as Liam continues to glance around, probably wondering if they're in a bearded cult.

"Those pricks left me out there before I realized it. Next thing I know, there was a cub, and a likely momma cougar, and gunshots, and I climbed the nearest tree."

Benson tenses, but the rest of the table snickers. Well, not Aunt Penny.

"I've told you to stop going out into the woods with those two!" she snaps.

They wouldn't have left me alone if they'd known there was a cougar, but I sure as hell don't defend them. They were just trying to get out of sawing a tree down for me.

The chainsaw is messed up, so it was going to have to be done the hard way. No one in this town is stupid enough to lend them anything of theirs, so borrowing a chainsaw was out of the question.

"I'll come build your bed," Benson offers.

He usually ends up fixing whatever they've broken, since they tend to do a shitty job at fixing it themselves. Not that they can't fix it, it's just the fact they love to annoy me to the fullest extent.

I grin while leaning against him a little more. He always smells so good. "Thanks, but I'm going to make them do it. They broke it, after all."

He narrows his eyes at me, and I mimic the motion. He rolls those eyes before looking back down at his plate, and I push my food aside as I finish eating.

"I notice I have a distinct lack of facial hair," Liam says, eyeing the fifteen or so other men. Yes, it's me, Aunt Penny, one baby-smooth skin Liam, and fifteen-ish beards.

"Get used to it," I grumble. "I was fifteen when this started," I add, gesturing to everyone, and once again tugging on Benson's beard, ignoring the sting when he reaches back and pinches my side in punishment. "That was nine years ago."

"When what started?" Liam asks curiously.

"The beards. All the fucking beards," I groan. "It's a town-wide challenge. The first one to cut their beard has to swim naked across the lake during the summer. That lake stays cold. Like really, really cold. Even in the summer." I gesture around like I'm pointing to the current season we're in. "So they all look like mountain men."

Benson chuckles, and I roll my eyes.

"You all grew those for a challenge?" Liam asks, pointing at some of the hideous bushes they wear with pride.

"A true Tomahawk man never backs down from a licensed challenge," my uncle says with an affirmative nod.

A few grunts follow that, also sounding affirmative.

I half expect the men around the table to start beating their chests like gorillas at any moment.

"*Licensed* challenge?"

No one answers that, because, well, Liam is an outsider, after all.

"They'd rather their faces look too similar to Sasquatch than worry about bothersome things such as ever getting laid again."

"I get laid," Tim pipes up.

"You're married," I deadpan. "And God bless your wife."

They all chuckle.

"So I have to grow a beard?" Liam asks, his lips twitching.

"No. It doesn't apply to anyone who comes in now. Not that it matters. Only one person comes to live here every ten years or so. But it seems like it doesn't matter to the now corrupted young ones either. A guy hits puberty, and he joins in on the challenge, even though it's years' old."

I glare at my uncle, the douche nozzle who instated the challenge and put it to a vote with the committee. He flashes a toothy grin at me through his beard.

"Did I mention I hate beards?" I add.

Benson bristles beside me.

"Your pretty, smooth face will be very much sought after," I tell Liam.

Again, Benson bristles.

Liam smirks before shrugging. He's cute, but neither of us is interested in the other, and there's zero chemistry between us. I'm cool with that, even though it's terribly tragic to pass up such a perfectly smooth face that would feel good to rub all over.

I burrow into Benson a little better as I try to pinpoint what's not working for me with Liam.

My girly parts haven't perked up and paid attention to him, so it's their own fault they're being deprived such a beautiful specimen.

"All the smart girls love beards," Paul says across from us. We went to school together, yet he looks like he's ten years older — because of the unkempt beard.

"Ha! Yeah. I'm sure that's why all the single women — myself included — don't touch the scraggly beards here. You guys don't even trim them. You can barely see your eyes. It's not enticing."

"No trimming allowed," my uncle goes on. "Not until someone loses."

"To be fair," Paul inserts, "no one thought the challenge would last this long. I was fifteen when it started. I'm twenty-four now."

I look to Liam, while still leaning against Benson, who is now a little stiffer than usual. Maybe he's mad about me insulting the beards.

Despite what they say, they've all gotten attached to the unruly wiry hair on their faces.

"I can remember my fifteen-year-old brothers standing in front of the mirror and willing their beards to grow. It was just patchy stubble for the first few years for them, but they were in it to win it."

"So you're telling me the women —"

"All twenty of us who aren't married and under the age of fifty," I butt in.

" —are so shallow as to not like us because of the beards?" Joey—a guy two years older than me—asks as he strokes that long, blond beard.

"We're not shallow for expecting normal grooming habits," I point out. "You can't see anything but a lot of beard. We don't even know what half of you look like."

"That's shallow," Paul pipes in.

"No. It's not. It's not unreasonable to ask you to trim the damn thing. Would you want to touch a girl who had hairy legs she showed off with pride? Legs so hairy that you could hide popcorn in them?"

They all give a full body shudder, including Benson.

Benson has grown unusually quiet. Well, not unusually. He's always quiet unless it's just the two of us, but he's also staring down at his food.

"Duck Dynasty guys have hot wives," Paul declares like he's starting a debate, holding his fork toward me, and deliberately not answering the hairy legs question.

Double standard, if you ask me. I have to shave my legs daily during the summer. No one sees them in the winter, so the shaving becomes more sporadic then. But you still can't lose popcorn in them, damn it.

"They were married before the beards, and their wives loved them. It'd be shallow to leave because of a beard." I tap my chin. "What about a girl with hairy armpits? The hair would be long enough to braid. Could you find her attractive?"

No one answers, but again, they all shudder in disgust.

That's what I thought.

"The point is, you expect women to groom our freaking limbs, yet you think we're all supposed to overlook the fact your *face* is a complete mystery, because it's heavily guarded by that brush pile you all call beards. Who wants to grind on a face like that?"

They all look to my uncle just as Aunt Penny tugs his beard. "I love the beard," she coos. "And I grind all over it all the time."

Just...*ew*.

"She was married pre-beard too," I say just as a bunch of accusing beards swing my way. "And in love prior to the beard. He could grow a gnarly hunch on his chest, and she'd pet it, thinking it was adorable."

It's true. They're still sickeningly in love.

My uncle grins at her and tugs her closer. At least I think he's grinning. Always hard to tell because...beard.

A few mumblings go on after that, and I sink against Benson's side, growing increasingly tired now that the adrenaline from the cougar episode is wearing off.

"So how long have you two known each other?" Liam asks, gesturing toward me and Benson as I fight to keep my eyes open.

Benson, who's been quiet until now, shifts his arm and turns his body so that I can lean against his chest and get more comfortable. His arm comes around my waist, tugging me closer when I start to sag.

"Since I was twenty-one," he says gruffly.

"Which was how long ago?" Liam lets the question trail off.

"He inherited his family's vacation cabin across the lake that they rented out but never stayed in but on occasion," my aunt supplies. "When he was eighteen, that is. But he kept to himself for the first year or two. I think…how old were you when you met Benson?" she asks, looking over at me.

I force my eyes to open wider. "Eighteen. Like he said, he was twenty-one. He was already bearded. The challenge had been going on for three years," I say around a yawn.

"I didn't know she existed before then," Benson says with a shrug.

"I spent a year in Seattle," I explain. "Learning graphic design. I graduated from school early — at seventeen — and lived with a friend of my mother's for a year until I turned eighteen and came back home. But we didn't become real friends until three years ago."

Liam nods and looks to Benson. "And what do you do?"

Everyone looks at Benson. Even I tilt my head back, looking up at him with a grin. He grunts and looks down at me before looking away, squeezing me to him a little more.

"No one knows," I say with a smile, returning my gaze to Liam. "At least, no one knows what he does for money."

"What do you do?" Benson volleys, glancing over at Liam.

Liam's lips twitch. "I should get going. I still have to unpack. Thank you, Penny, for the invite. It was nice to meet my neighbors."

"Where are you staying?" I ask, feeling Benson tense again.

What's with him?

His arm tightens around my waist, and I study Liam beside us.

"I bought the Morris cabin."

My jaw falls open. The Morris cabin is just as big, if not bigger, than the ridiculously huge cabin Benson owns. Both are like cabin wet dreams.

Sometimes I spend the night in Benson's cabin just to be spending the night in Benson's cabin. Because I love it. It's awesome.

"That's about a mile from me," I note. "Same side of the lake."

He grins, Benson mutters something, and Liam stands, bidding everyone farewell.

"Come on," Benson says, lifting me with him as he stands.

My feet hit the ground, and I glance back as all the men start covering the leftovers and cleaning up for Aunt Penny.

"I'll get you home," Benson informs me with that no-nonsense tone of his. "And I'll have a talk with your brothers."

"You gonna club them over the head with your beard? Because I'd watch that. Might even change my stance on beards."

He shakes his head, his arm going around my shoulders, and we leave the partiers behind as he tosses his rifle over his back, the strap coming across his shoulder.

Benson is a big guy. Not in the chubby way. Even in the summer he wears jeans, and he always has on a loose shirt. His arms are solid, but not overly muscular.

I really like his arms. They're totally arm porn material.

He's tall. Like 6'3 or so. That's what I mean by big.

I glance back, seeing Liam board his fancy bass boat, and note he's about the same height.

"You into him?" Benson asks, noticing my line of view.

17

h. Too pretty."

He snorts derisively.

"So beards are too ugly, but smooth faces are too pretty. In other words, you can't be satisfied."

I elbow him in the ribs, and he tugs me closer.

"He's model pretty," I go on. "Saw plenty of the like in Seattle. Didn't do anything for me then either. Guys like that are fun for a minute, but they never settle down."

"Thought you didn't want to settle down. That's what you keep telling Penny."

Yeah. I totally just stepped into that shit pile, didn't I? Must've been something in that food.

"I don't. But I also don't want to be used and treated with the same respect a blowup doll gets either."

He looks down at me like he's studying me, then shakes his head and focuses back on the trail. The bass boat blares by us, and I offer a wave to Liam as he passes us.

"Why didn't you just drive me over on your boat?" I ask Benson.

"Because your dock needs to be fixed before I dock there again. I'll come work on it next week."

"You don't have to. I can get those dicks to do something. It's their dock too."

"They're the reason it needs to be fixed," he says, sounding a little angry.

"They'll fix it. They always do," I say around another yawn.

"And then I always re-fix it. Might as well cut out the middle man."

I don't bother arguing.

Right as we get to the cabin, I decide I'm really going to kill my brothers. All my underwear is hanging from my porch, on tiny little nails, and dangling.

Benson practically turns to stone.

"What the hell?" he asks.

"They're dead," I bite out.

"Why would they — "

"Because I burned all theirs after they wrecked my bed."

"But why would they — "

I turn to face him. "Because bugs, Benson. *Bugs*. I'll be too freaked out to ever wear those again, because…bugs."

I shudder dramatically, and he arches an eyebrow. Do you have any idea how many places bugs can hide? Or how small they are so as not to be noticed?

My vagina is sacred!

"Guess I won't be wearing panties for a while," I say on a sigh.

For some reason, Benson drops his rifle.

Chapter 2

Wild Ones Tip #115
Never trust a Wild One unless you're a fan of
reckless endangerment.

LILAH

My two dark-haired, bushy-bearded brothers are blinking at me innocently as I berate them for over an hour. Benson talked to them before he left last night, and so they built my bed today.

All day.

They kept me out until it was finished.

Only...

"This bed takes up my entire room! I don't even have a mattress to fit it! I asked for a double."

They continue to stare at me with wide-eyed innocence.

"Fix it!"

It happens too fast for me to stop it. Suddenly, they're up and out my door, a fog of laughter in their wake.

I'm going to kill them.

I'm not sleeping on my mattress when it's on the floor. I get a little freaked out. I know it's irrational, but I feel like I'm more accessible to bugs if I'm on the floor.

I can't sleep on my couch. Last time I tried that, I woke up sore all over. It's not even comfortable to sit on anymore. It was a hand-me-down from someone else, who got it as a hand-me-down from someone, who also got it as —

You get the idea. This couch has been around since listening to Elvis was considered scandalous and poodle skirts were all the craze.

My one-bedroom cabin has no other options, and I grumble while walking out the door. I'm sleeping in a bed, damn it. And not Aunt Penny's guest bed, because she and my uncle have been hella loud since I can remember.

I'm still traumatized from hearing their sounds.

After our parents died, we moved in with them. At fifteen. The year the beard challenge began.

I often think the beard challenge was to give my brothers something to focus on other than the ache we all had. It seemed to work.

My aunt and uncle were thoughtful and considerate for a year, knowing we'd suffered a loss, which, so had Aunt Penny. My mother was her twin.

But after that year, they seemed to forget we could hear them fucking for ten miles away.

No thank you.

Instead, I walk on my creaky dock, untie my boat, and carefully climb down, praying it doesn't collapse — the dock, I mean.

And I drive across the lake to Benson's beast of a home. He has five extra rooms, and all of them have comfy beds. He has family come once a year, but I never see them.

No one does.

They stay at the cabin, and Benson doesn't invite anyone over. The lake is big enough that you can't see faces from across it either, at least not without the help of binoculars.

Yes, I've used them. I'm curious, so what?

Never seen more than a glimpse of the elusive Nolans family since I never know the *exact* time of their arrival. Benson just goes dark, and the town knows his family is in.

He even ignores *me* when they're here, and I'm his best friend. The second they're gone, he's at my house, picking me up, and taking me fishing or something. And he never talks about them at all. Trust me, I've tried to pry.

It makes me suspicious…sort of like everything.

I dock my boat, tie it off, and walk up the fifteen steps to his door. I bang on it for several minutes before it swings open, and Benson arches an eyebrow when he sees me.

"What have they done now?" he asks.

I love his voice. It's always so smooth and deep, but not creepy deep. In fact, it's that sexy deep that I used to react to. Total voice porn. I've trained my body against it. Mostly.

Because it's Benson. My mysterious friend Benson.

The guy I need in my life to keep me sane and doesn't mind being in my corner of crazy.

"My bed's too big for my mattress, and my couch isn't any more comfortable than it has been all week. If I don't get some quality sleep, I may kill someone, starting with the two anus leeches who caused this debacle. Can I borrow a room for the night?"

He steps back.

"You know you can. You should have come sooner."

He's in a T-shirt and sweat pants. The sweats look like quality sweats too. As though he went high-end. He always looks so different at home than when he's outside with all our friends.

Obviously I don't mention it aloud. As I said, he never tells me anything.

"I'll come fix your bed tomorrow. They're just doing it to irk you now," he goes on.

"No need," I say sleepily. "I've got something planned. Something major. I'll be staying here after I do it, because I'll need your protection."

He laughs under his breath. "My protection?"

I nod as he follows me up the stairs. "Which room?" I ask as he pulls me away from the wall I've leaned against and started falling asleep on.

His arms reach down and lift me like I'm weightless, and he cradles me to him as he finishes carrying me up the stairs. I really love how he smells.

Always have.

It's comforting and refreshing, and…Benson.

I'm really tired.

The last thing I remember is touching something soft, my body being covered, and something suspiciously resembling a tickling kiss is pressed to my head.

The next thing I know, I'm waking up to bright sunshine and the sound of pans rattling. My body feels as rejuvenated as I feel. I don't know why I didn't crash here sooner.

What has me stumbling over my feet as I head downstairs and into the kitchen, is the sight of Benson in a tight, black tank. Holy shit. Where's he been hiding that body?

His shoulders are broad and sculpted. His waist is tapered perfectly, which is showcased by the tight-fitted shirt. All that arm porn is twice as sexy today, because you can see more of it.

Suddenly, I feel self-conscious, because my hair is a mess, my flannel bottoms are five years old, and my T-shirt has a picture of a pink mammoth on it.

He's cooking. A body like that is already distracting. And he's *cooking*.

"Hungry?" he asks, and I debate the meaning of that word.

I am *not* gawking at Benson like I want a bite. No way.

Where's his oversized T-shirt?!

My eyes snap up to meet his, but he's just staring at me blankly, like he didn't notice I was practically wetting my non-existent panties for him.

"Very," I say tightly.

Apparently my sex drought is fucking with my head.

"So what's this plan of revenge you need my protection for? You passed out before giving me answers," he says, cracking some eggs in a skillet.

I move in beside him to take over frying the bacon, acting like this is our normal routine.

When my arm brushes his, I shudder. What is wrong with me?

I'm reacting more to him than I did the pretty boy. Surely I'm not being conditioned to overlook the unruly beard. Is this brainwash or something?

"Can't tell you. You might stop me."

I feel his smile.

"Doubtful. Spill."

"If you'll tell me how you ended up in Tomahawk, I'll share my awesome plan with you."

I arch an eyebrow at him, and he shakes his head, careful to keep his long beard away from the skillet.

"You know how I ended up here."

"I know you got your family's cabin, but not why you came to live here. You're a mystery, Benson Nolans. Like, what do you do for a living? How did your family afford to just give this to you? And why come to stay in the middle of nowhere?"

He shrugs. "Needed the change, and I can't tell you what I do, because this is Tomahawk."

I give him a bland look. "You can't tell me what you do because this is Tomahawk," I repeat.

He nods, but I feel him smirking, even though that beard disguises it.

I roll my eyes.

"Not sure what that means."

"Tomahawk expects certain things from its men. Best if I keep my secrets a secret."

"What about your family? Why can't any of us ever meet them?"

"Because this is Tomahawk," he says again.

"Then you don't get to learn my plan of revenge," I say with a smile.

"Why?" he drawls, leaning closer to me to push my hair over my shoulder.

I do not shiver. Nope. Not at all.

Okay, maybe a tiny shiver. He's a damn good-smelling man. I'm a sex-deprived woman. Shit happens.

"Because this is Tomahawk," I tell him with a smirk of my own.

He rolls his eyes and resumes making breakfast.

As soon as we're done, we make our own plates and head to his table, sitting across from each other. We eat in relative silence, and I stare at anything but the body he's showing off. Why is he wearing a tank? He never wears a tight shirt. And it's driving me out of my mind.

"Do you ever date?" I ask curiously.

"Occasionally," he says, looking down at his phone.

"Define *occasionally*."

Wouldn't I have heard about someone dating Benson? Wouldn't he have told me? He spends most of his free time with me, so obviously I should know if he's dating. I know all the single women.

Why are my nails pressing into my palms just thinking of another woman touching him?

Again, I have issues.

"I dated someone for a while, came to live here, then dated a little here and there when I went home to visit." He shrugs.

"But no one from here?"

His eyes come up to meet mine as his eyebrows raise. "Why the inquisition into my dating life?"

"Just realizing I've never seen you with a woman."

He grins. "Never had one out here besides you. At least not one that wasn't related to me."

He looks back down at his phone. He never studies his phone like that, so what's going on? Why do I feel obsessed right now? Why is he being so suspicious? Or am I the suspicious one?

"So you leave Tomahawk to go back to…wherever…and date when you're not here?"

He shrugs noncommittally, still staring at his phone.

"Girls here not good enough for you?" I ask, unsure why I'm stabbing my eggs a little harder than necessary.

"Heard they don't like the beard," he says, even though he sounds a little annoyed by that.

"Then cut the beard."

"I'm not swimming across that godforsaken lake." He shudders, not lifting his eyes to meet mine.

His phone goes off, and he stands. "Gotta get this. I'll see you later if you really do need my protection," he tells me without a backward glance.

Apparently I've been dismissed. Usually happens when I ask too many personal questions. Benson is a private guy, after all. He never gives more answers than he wants to. He's lived here for years, and that's all the information we have on him.

I'm his closest friend and still have no clue about who he was before he came to Tomahawk.

I finish eating and then take the time to wash up the plates. Benson never returns, so I let myself out and drive my boat back toward my place…but I notice my new neighbor down the lake on his dock.

It's not surprising to see he's well-built. It *is* surprising to see him shirtless as he hammers away on his dock. Deciding I can't execute my plan until nightfall, I drive toward his dock.

I wonder if Delaney has seen him yet.

Making a mental note to drive out and get Delaney sometime soon, I pull up to his dock. He looks up, smiling when he sees it's me, and wipes sweat off his brow.

He really is pretty.

Yet my girly parts are still dormant.

Funny, they seemed to be riled up this morning. I assumed they were ready to come out of hibernation.

But, despite the gorgeous male specimen in front of me, I'm still not having the appropriate reaction.

Figures.

"Hidey, neighbor," he says with a mock southern drawl.

I quirk an eyebrow at him, and he flashes me that perfect smile. "Sorry," he says, chuckling. "Always wanted to say that."

He comes to help me tie off my boat, and I haul myself onto his dock, wondering if our backwoods accents sound southern to him or something.

"I take it you didn't have neighbors at your last place?" I ask, prying.

"Had tons of them. I lived in LA. But you don't really talk to your neighbors in LA, at least not the part where I lived. Then I moved to a more upscale home on the outskirts, and had no close neighbors there."

He shrugs one shoulder as he moves back to his spot to kneel down and start prying an old board loose. My eyebrows go up in surprise.

"Why wouldn't you tell us where you came from yesterday, yet have no problem with it today?"

"The company yesterday was intimidating. I mean, they've been growing beards for years because they're too 'manly' to back down from a challenge. Didn't figure they'd take too kindly to the new city guy, and didn't want to paint a target on my back. Can you keep a secret?" he asks, that grin still blinding.

"No problem. So why the move?"

"Got tired of city life," he says with another shrug, then goes back to hammering a new board. "Decided to come somewhere more remote. My realtor sent me this place as a possibility, and I fell in love with the cabin. I've always loved working with wood, so this gives me a chance to actually do it in nature."

Yes, I could totally make half a dozen dirty jokes about him 'loving working with wood' and 'actually doing it in nature,' but I suppress my inner teenage boy and focus on the important part.

In five minutes, I know more about him than Benson. Well, about his past. I still find Liam suspicious. Just as I do all newbies.

"Just wake up?" he muses, looking me over.

I grimace, remembering I still haven't seen a mirror or touched a brush. "Rough night," I vaguely answer.

He grins again, then resumes hammering away.

I open my mouth to say something else, when the loud motor of a boat roars closer, and I turn, seeing Benson driving this way on his boat.

"Your boyfriend still pissed that your aunt tried setting us up with him right there?" Liam asks as I cut my eyes away from the approaching Benson.

"He's not my boyfriend."

He continues smiling down at that nail he must find amusing.

"Sure didn't act that way yesterday," he says.

Before I can correct him, Benson is coasting to the end of the dock.

29

"You forgot this," Benson says, holding up my bra as a grin cracks through that beard.

Liam chuckles, and I narrow my eyes at the bearded man at the end. That bra has probably been at his house for two weeks, because I wasn't wearing a bra last night.

"Just toss it in my boat."

He does, and it lands directly in my seat. My boat is just a little flat-bottom thing with a motor Benson installed for me three years ago. Nothing flashy like they have.

"You coming back over tonight?" Benson asks, making this sound far more scandalous than it is.

He's in his standard jeans and loose T-shirt now, so I'm thinking a little clearer.

"Probably," I say, not bothering to make this seem like it's not what Benson is implying, and giving him the satisfaction of seeing me defensive.

I genuinely don't care if Liam gets the wrong idea, so no need in scrambling around like a fool to clarify things. Besides, for some reason, it wouldn't feel right to deny it in front of Benson, almost as if I was wronging him on some level.

Which is stupid. We're friends.

I'm not sure why he's playing this game, but I still feel like I should be on his side of it.

I tend to overthink things and come up with a thousand different reasons for why things are going on, in case you haven't noticed.

I end up convincing myself that Benson wants me to defend myself, and that's the real reason I'm not. Because it's obviously better than the alternative that I'm starting to notice him as more than a beard.

That's terrifying.

I'm the head of the anti-beard committee, after all. We've been protesting this damn challenge since it started.

Hey, it's Tomahawk. We don't have much else to do.

Benson winks at me before pushing away from the dock and restarting his motor, driving toward town.

We have roads, but it's usually quicker to boat to town from his side of the lake.

My eyes turn back to see a sly grin on Liam's face. "Not your boyfriend, huh?"

Again, it still feels wrong to correct him. Why? Beats me. I blame it on the distinct lack of caffeine this morning.

I talk to Liam about the town, telling him how it works and explaining some random things, keeping all the conversation topics safe. Just as I'm filling him in on how spread out all the neighbors are, another motor revs, coming closer.

I smirk when I see Delaney driving this way, waving at me as she nears. I guess I don't have to fetch her after all.

I also notice a few other familiar faces too, and then see a few cars pulling into Liam's house.

I flash him a grin when confusion mars his face.

"Welcome to Tomahawk," I tell him as women start walking down the bank, covered dishes in their hands. "The land of a hundred unruly beards, and everyone's own individual brand of crazy. You're officially the most eligible, baby-face bachelor."

Delaney barely even says *hi* to me as she shoves her way to the front of the line, and I hop on my boat, ready to get away while I still can. Besides, it'll free up space for another boat to tie off.

"I...uh...I," Liam says, gesturing for help as five women talk over him, trying to introduce themselves.

Grinning, I drive away, leaving him to fend for himself as I head to my cabin.

I notice a few of the guys fishing on the lake, staring over at Liam's home that is being swarmed with more and more women. Paul is among the crowd, and he tosses his hat into the lake, looking annoyed.

I shoot him an I-told-you-so look, and he flips me off as I laugh and coast up to my dock. I'll be glad when my brothers get my lift fixed. The lift they tore up with their boat that was way too big for it.

I step over the few shady boards they jacked up during the lift-breaking debacle, and head toward my cabin to shower and change for the day.

Tonight is when the magic happens.

So I pack a bag.

I'll be staying with Benson for at least two nights.

Chapter 3

Wild Ones Tip #111
Always bring backup and snacks.
Never know when you'll need snacks.

LILAH

*S*nip.

Slow breaths.

Snip. That sound is almost deafening in this otherwise silent room, sans the occasional snore.

Snip.

I cringe when a leg moves, and my breath goes completely silent, because I'm holding it.

Snip.

A hand darts up, grabbing my wrist, before a set of eyes open in confusion.

"Go to sleep. Go to sleep. Go to sleep, little baby," I sing, obviously panicking when my heart starts hammering in my chest.

The singing doesn't work.

Killian bolts upright in bed and flips on the lamp, which rouses Hale from his sleep. Their beds are a few feet apart, since I sort of moved the bed there earlier, knowing they'd be too lazy to move it back to Hale's room before crashing for the night.

I had a plan, and they're wrecking it by waking up.

My brothers look at me in confusion, then at the scissors in my hand, then at the hair on the floor.

Carefully, while they're still utterly baffled and just-woken from sleep, I put the scissors down calmly, back toward the door, grab the camera I have set up and ease it into my backpack, and…run like a maniac.

"Holy fucking shit!" I hear Hale snap, just as I leap off their front porch. Tucking and rolling back up to my feet, I race like my life depends on it to the boats.

"Lilah!" Killian roars, but I giggle like a crazed woman as I leap onto my boat that only has one rope tying it off, and quickly get going before can get to me.

I'm halfway across the water when I hear their boat roar to life.

Their boat is bigger and faster, so I drive like hell to Benson's dock, half-ass tie off.

"Benson!" My shrill scream sounds so foreign and unlike me, as my legs pump like an Olympian again.

"Benson!" I squeal again when I hear the boat docking behind me.

"Get her!" Killian roars.

"Get back here, Lilah!" Hale shouts, furious.

Yeah, like that's going to work. Nope. I run that much harder.

The door to Benson's home swings open just as I hurl myself up the fifteenth step, and I leap into his arms, wrapping my legs around his waist, my arms around his neck, and cling to him like a shameless spider monkey.

I'm vaguely aware of the fact his hands immediately go to my ass, squeezing it, and I'm also vaguely aware of the fact those dormant girl parts are definitely taking notice. In fact, if it wasn't for the rebel yell coming from behind me, I'd have to study this a little more intently.

"What the—"

Benson's words cut off, and his hands immediately leave my ass.

"Don't even think about it. I'll beat the hell out of both of you," he cautions, turning and depositing me onto the floor.

I peek around the wall that's now shielding me, seeing my brothers as they seethe, spitting mad. Here's the thing, Benson Nolans happens to be a black belt. We only know this because he has his belts framed, and he does this spinning kick thingy that totally makes him a badass.

He's the one guy in Tomahawk who can kick Killian's ass, even though Killian is a mean fighter with a nasty right hook.

"This is between us and her. Look what she fucking did!" Hale roars.

They both point to their patchy, messed up, mostly clipped beards, and I snicker to myself as Benson works hard against his own laugh.

"Guess the beard challenge is finally over," Benson says, amused.

"No!" my brothers shout in unison.

"She did this! Not us. We can't lose by default!" Hale adds.

"Nowhere does it state that you have to trim it yourself to be the loser. Just says it has to be trimmed," Benson says, his beard twitching.

"Then who did she cut first?" Killian demands.

"Same time! I have a video of it!" I pull my video camera from my backpack, and Benson takes it and puts it on a table next to the door, not looking at it.

"You can't be serious!" Hale growls.

I giggle like an idiot, staying safely tucked next to Black Belt Benson.

"You did break her bed *while* trying to steal her ceiling fan," Benson points out helpfully.

"But this is the beard challenge! Too far. Too fucking far," Killian barks.

"You also left her behind with a momma cougar." Benson sounds less amused and a little angrier about that.

I stand a little taller, primly smirking at my brothers.

"Didn't know there was a cougar when we left her, jackass. This would be deserved if we did."

Killian gestures to his mangled, uneven, horrible beard — or the remnants of it anyway.

"And you rebuilt her bed way too big for her mattress. You also wrecked her dock lift—since you never built your own dock—and then messed up the entire end of the dock when the lift crashed into the lake. You still haven't fixed that, by the way."

They both blink, then as one, glare at me like I've been tattling. I totally have been tattling.

"So you think this is justified?" Killian asks incredulously, shifting his gaze and staring at Benson as though he's an alien from outer space.

"I think it was just a matter of time before you pushed her too far."

"She pushes us too far too!" Hale snaps, pointing at me. "You act like she's an angel. In case you've forgotten, we're not the only heathens on this corner!"

"Take it up with your uncle. You're not touching Lilah."

They both narrow their eyes, and I confidently slide in next to Benson as he drops his arm to my shoulders. I'm practically gloating as I curl up against his side.

"This isn't over, sis. You'll have to come home sooner or later."

"If you touch her hair in any way, I'll shave you both bald and drag you across the lake daily for at least a month. Then I'll let your uncle take his turn," Benson threatens, and I grin a little bigger, while simultaneously getting a little sick.

I never considered they might come after my hair.

The Wild Women are serious about one thing—hair. Why? Well, that's a long story.

My hair is long, dark, and I've worked damn hard to keep it healthy at this length. As if thinking about it, Benson runs his fingers through it absently, still staring down my brothers.

I'm not sure why that feels so intimate, but it does.

"Fine," Killian snarls, but I still don't trust them not to touch my hair.

My hair!

There are only so many ways to stay feminine when you have to live in the wilderness. My hair is one thing that reminds me I'm a girl most days.

Well, that and my vagina.

I don't let the hair grow long there, in case you're wondering.

"Get home. I'll call your uncle," Benson says dismissively.

They both threaten me one last time before stalking off, and Benson shuts the door as I step back. I blow out a relieved breath, until he turns to look at me with exasperation.

"Are you serious? The beards? You went for the beards?" he groans.

"This is why I didn't tell you my plan," I state dryly, defiantly crossing my arms over my chest.

His eyes dip to register the motion, and he swallows as he presumably loses his train of thought. I have no idea why I decided to come over here in a skimpy little pajama set.

It's midnight now. I should look like death, per the usual. Not like a sex kitten.

Yesterday I looked like a hobo. I didn't want to be so unappealing tonight, and don't ask me why. I'm suffering some confusion at the moment.

His eyes drift down my legs that have a touch of tan on them. And they're smooth, because unlike the men in this town, I use a razor.

My camisole top barely covers anything, and even shows off a sliver of skin of my stomach. It's not completely flat, but it's mostly flat. Flat enough to show off. It's also a little too chilly out there to be dressed like this.

Even in my head, I'm trying to justify my mostly indecent and completely impractical wardrobe choice. Damn Benson. What's he doing to me?

His eyes snap back up to meet mine.

"You decided to get revenge dressed like that?" He gestures to...all of me.

"Easier to run in," I lie.

Either he buys the lie, or just doesn't care enough to press for more. He walks by me, heading to his den.

"I figured you'd changed your mind about coming over when you didn't show up. Now I realize you were just waiting on them to be dead to the world."

I remove my boots, thinking back on all the poor logic in my plan. Both of them waking up *while* I was cutting their beards was *not* part of the plan. That almost caused cardiac arrest.

"I was really hoping you were still awake," I say on a sigh. "I should have told you it'd be late."

"You're going to need to stay here for more than a night."

I nod, agreeing. They're way more pissed than even I expected.

And I'm not losing my hair, damn it.

Benson drops to the couch, stretching one long leg to his coffee table, before hitting play on the TV. I go to curl up right against his side, and don't think about it until after he goes stiff.

Seriously. What is wrong with me?

We always touch, but I'm practically all over him right now.

His arm comes around my shoulders, and I stop thinking. If I'm attracted to a guy with a beard, then I'll never hear the end of it. I'm okay with that.

But…Benson. I can't do that with Benson.

First of all, he doesn't date girls around here. Secondly, he's a friend. One of my best friends, oddly enough.

I need to stop having weird reactions to him.

"You tired?" he asks, shifting so that I'm even closer, practically on top of his side.

"No. I will be when the adrenaline wears off though."

He laughs softly, his arm growing more relaxed around me.

"You need your laptop?" he asks.

"It's in my bag." I gesture to the abandoned backpack near the door. "I made sure to pack the essentials, just in case."

"Good thinking," he says, a smile to his voice.

"Thanks for the protection."

"You'll owe me after this is all over. They're pissed now, but wait until tomorrow."

A grin forms on my lips as the adrenaline slowly wears off. I'm not sure when it happens, but at some point I feel him shifting again, and before I know it, he's nothing more than a pillow under me.

Chapter 4

Wild Ones Tip #327
Always watch your back. Or at least have someone crazy
enough to watch it for you.

LILAH

I jolt awake to the loud blaring of music, and arms tighten around my waist as Benson wakes up too.

Yep. I slept on top of Benson.

I'm not going to lie; I'm very tempted to grind against him right now, because he totally has morning wood, and it's pressed right against the vee of my thighs. My thighs that are spread shamelessly over him, because somehow I straddled him in my sleep.

I sit up, and he takes a second to look at me, confused, then down to where I'm straddling his lap, and back up to my eyes. He scrubs his face as that music starts playing again, and he looks over to where it's coming from.

Stupid phone.

We're together all the time, and I rarely see that phone. Now, in a matter of days, I've seen it constantly.

He grabs it, putting a hand on my hip when I try to get up. I stay put instead of moving as he answers.

"Bill," he says, his voice causing me to inwardly moan.

Why does he sound so sexy right now?

That beard…does nothing for me. Yet it's taking all my strength not to pull his pants down and relieve the ache he's left me with.

It doesn't make sense. I didn't have any reaction at all to Liam.

And he's gorgeous!

Yet Benson has me physically aching.

Wait…Bill? Uncle Bill?

Quickest libido killer in history.

Benson smiles as he sits up, still keeping me in his lap.

"Yeah. She's here. Spent the night after the guys chased after her." He looks at me and winks, and I get more comfortable on his lap, maybe wiggling more than necessary.

That has him tensing.

Talk about mixed signals.

"We'll head right over."

I get up as he puts his phone away. "Your uncle is calling a meeting at his house," he says as he stands.

"Right now?"

"Apparently we were the last to be called. Half the people are over there now, so yeah," he says, running his fingers through his shaggy, black hair. "Now."

I grab my backpack, cursing myself when I see I packed a lot of sleeping things, but nothing to wear. Deciding not to give a damn, I grab my toothbrush, hairbrush, and a ponytail holder, and rush upstairs behind Benson.

He barely turns around when I follow him into the bathroom.

"What're you doing?"

"Brushing my teeth and pulling my hair up," I say as he turns away from me like he's hiding something.

"I have to piss."

Oh. Yeah.

I blush and dart out, and I run to another bathroom down the hall, wondering why I'm suddenly following him around.

I brush my teeth quickly, comb through my hair, then pull it up before jogging back out. Benson is walking down the stairs as I tug on my boots.

"You're going like that?" he asks incredulously.

What's wrong with what I'm wearing? He's in his typical jeans and tee. I'm in pajamas. Who cares? It's Tomahawk.

"But you're not even wearing a bra. And those shorts…are you seriously not wearing any underwear?"

"Bugs, remember? I won't ever wear them again until I get new ones. Those little beasts can hide anywhere."

"Those shorts are really short—"

"Hurry! I have to see them swim the lake," I tell him, tying the last shoe string on my boot.

"You remember that half the guys are not getting sex regularly, right?" he drawls as he follows me down the stairs to the dock.

"What does that have to do with my brothers swimming the lake?" I retort, staring at him like he's lost his mind.

He stares back at me for a second like I'm an idiot, but I have no idea what I'm missing.

"Nothing," he grumbles, finally helping me into his boat.

I'm practically bouncing with excitement as he unties us and starts the motor, getting us away from his dock before driving us toward my uncle's.

I swivel in my seat to face him, noticing how tense he looks. "What's wrong?" I ask, making my voice carry over the steady roar of the motor.

"I'm just curious what he's going to do," he says.

"Uncle Bill?"

He nods, but before I can ask more questions, we're coasting up to the dock that is already teeming with other boats. It's a massive dock, since my aunt hosts parties all the time.

I help Benson tie off, and he lifts me out of the boat until I can get my knees under me and stand. Then he hauls himself onto the high dock. His hand snakes around my waist, tugging me to him when we see Liam climbing up onto the dock as well.

"Sorry for imposing, but when Penny called, I figured I had to come bear witness to the 'biggest upset in Tomahawk history.' How can a guy pass that up?" Liam asks, smiling over at me before flicking his gaze back to Benson.

"Should be interesting," Benson says gruffly, his grip tightening on me even more as he hurries us by Liam.

"Those are some really nice…boots," I hear Liam say from behind me.

"Thanks," I say, walking a little taller in my girly combat boots with pink shoe strings.

Rarely ever does anyone notice my boots. After all, Kylie Malone is the one with a massive collection of pretty boots, so mine get overlooked.

"You have no idea what you're doing, do you?" Benson grumbles.

"Huh?"

He doesn't answer. Instead, he keeps me pressed to his side as we walk toward the assembly. Paul turns to look back at us, then turns to face my uncle as he talks. Then he whips his head back around, eyes wide and fixed on me as he stumbles to get the rest of his body turned around.

Benson mutters something too low for me to hear, and he moves in behind me, before wrapping his arms around my waist. I have no idea why he's acting so weird.

I don't usually wear my pajamas in public, but it's not like it's a big deal or offensive. These guys wear the same clothes for days sometimes. Not Benson, but most of them. And for fuck's sake, have you seen the beards?

"Hey, Lilah," Paul drawls as my uncle talks about who is missing.

He waggles his eyebrows at me, and Benson's fists clench against my middle.

"Hey, weirdo. What's wrong with your eyebrows?" I ask seriously.

Paul's beard sags, and I assume he's frowning, as Benson snorts.

"That was my sexy look," Paul defends.

"Have you seen your face? Any expression is hidden under all that wiry hair. And why the hell are you even trying to shoot me sexy looks, anyway? You don't even like me."

His eyes drop to my legs again, then back up to meet my gaze. "I've changed my mind."

Benson, bless him, tells Paul to fuck off.

"There she is!" Killian snarls, pointing at me like I'm the town's leper.

I'm not gonna lie... I totally back against Benson and squeeze his hands that are covering my stomach, praying he protects me.

What if this turns into a bearded mob?

I like my hair, damn it.

My uncle's exasperated eyes meet mine.

"What were you thinking by interfering in the beard challenge?" he demands.

"There are no rules stating anything about interference," I say, pointing that out. I actually read the rules — yes, there's a list of rules.

"It's an unspoken rule," my uncle chides.

"This is just too entertaining," Liam says quietly from beside us, a grin playing on his lips.

"Well, it wasn't written. So technically, I didn't break any rules."

I still back into Benson even more, simply because my confidence isn't as sturdy as it was on the way over here. I never thought about this coming back on me.

Benson's arms tighten to the fullest extent, cocooning me in false security.

Aunt Penny smirks at me before rolling her eyes.

"I think we should put it to a vote to decide the course of action," Hale suggests, stepping beside my uncle and leveling me with a challenging glare.

"What vote?" Paul asks, bemused.

"To decide if the challenge is really over or not," my uncle declares, and my heart sinks.

I really wanted them to have to swim the lake.

"And to decide if our dear sister has to swim the lake in our place," Killian chimes in, smiling menacingly at me.

My uncle strokes his beard thoughtfully, as though he's actually considering that diabolical excuse for an idea.

"That's actually a good idea. It would give anyone else pause in the future, should they want to interfere as my niece has," my uncle, the traitor, decides.

Several men chatter, thinking it's a good idea.

"Or you could vote that the beard challenge is finally over, then you can all shave your faces and actually get laid," I quickly point out.

This has everyone's attention. Well, everyone who hasn't been getting any because...beard.

Some of them look to be considering it, and I glare at my asshole brothers, who show signs of worry now.

Unfortunately, given the chatter around us, I'm starting to think more people are leaning toward throwing me into the lake and making me swim it. "Fear the beard" starts to take on new meaning.

Even in the summer, the warmest that water gets is still too cold. They'll pull me out before I get hypothermic, but...I'd rather not reach that limit. Obviously.

As if by some divine intervention, five of the prettiest single women in town are suddenly crashing the beard party, and they practically swarm poor Liam. He casts a helpless glance in my direction, but I'm loving this.

It totally helps my cause. And I selfishly take pleasure in his torment.

"I vote we call the beard challenge over and the Vincent brothers swim the lake," Paul immediately chimes in, glaring at Liam as he struggles away from the women.

"I second that," Joey groans.

And the votes continue to fly in. My uncle doesn't look happy about it, and my brothers look even more furious.

"What says you, Benson?" my uncle grumbles.

"I vote the challenge is over. It's been long enough. Besides, they really deserve to swim the lake more than she does."

My uncle glances at me, shakes his head, then turns to my two brothers, who curse me as they walk the metaphorical plank, which is the dock.

They start stripping, and I keep my eyes up, because no sister wants to see her naked brothers. Some things just can't be unseen.

"Someone drive along beside them and pull them out when their lips turn blue if they don't make it across," Uncle Bill says, sighing as though he's devastated.

Liam is quick to volunteer to be the boat driver, and he sprints to his boat, leaving behind the five women.

"Benson, help him out," my uncle says.

Benson seems reluctant, but he releases me, walking out to follow Liam. He lets Liam drive as he takes a seat and shoots me an unknown look. Again, expressions are really hard to read around here because...beard.

Sick of hearing that? Well, I bet I'm sicker of all the unruly beards.

"You're welcome," Aunt Penny says as she joins me.

"You told the girls where to find Liam," I surmise.

"Figured your brothers would put it to that vote. They're decidedly predictable in this instance. A little visual encouragement on your behalf couldn't hurt, so, yes; I told the girls where the pretty bachelor would be."

"Thanks," I say on an appreciative sigh.

"Thank *you*. As much as I love the beard, I miss Bill's lips," she confesses on a groan.

I laugh as she winks at me. "By the way, Benson seems to be very protective of you. Always has been, but especially so since Liam came into town."

I shrug, trying to be cool. I'm not really sure what the deal is. I was totally into him this morning, but he seemed just as 'friend-zoned' as always when it came to me. So…yeah.

"I'd hate to ever mess up that friendship," I finally say.

She sighs as though that's the worst answer ever.

"I'm never going to get any babies," she says before moping off.

Sad fact: she wasn't able to have kids of her own. Which is why she always treated us like she was a surrogate mother, which she later came to be. She didn't even hesitate to take in three orphans that most people — even the saints — would have been horrified to face.

Three teenage Wild Ones.

Instead of dwelling on Benson issues — which are weird and untimely — I move to the edge to watch as my brothers yelp when they crash into the cold water. A grin beams across my face when they start swimming as fast as they can.

Pride, of course, has them hoping to make it to the other side of the lake before they have to be hauled out.

Man cards will be deducted authenticity points if they have to be pulled out. And they're Vincents, after all. The dead chipmunk flag flies on our corner for a reason. They have a reputation to uphold.

Benson and Liam follow behind them, and I ignore Paul when he asks me what I'm doing later.

It's just a pair of shorts. I've worn shorts before. Maybe not shorts so thin, but still…he's a weirdo.

I revel in the misery of my brothers as their whimpers echo back to me, and I grin in delight when they start swimming faster. I think I see their teeth chattering.

"My balls! They're trying to burrow up inside my stomach!" Hale groans.

"Mine are too numb to move. I'd better not lose them," Killian gripes.

"I better go get some clothes before they get back and kill me," I say to no one in particular, racing toward my cabin.

Running, though hated, is once again necessary. I quickly pack a few things, panting the entire time, and then dart out to realize…my boat is at Benson's.

My eyes dart over to where my brothers are almost to the other side. Damn, they're fast.

I race back to Aunt Penny's, and I jog inside to go change. And to hide. As soon as I'm done changing, I borrow the keys to her Jeep, and drive to town. Kylie Malone lives in town, and I run the chance of her being home.

Fortunately, her green beaver flag—*ha, no, don't make this dirty*—is flying, and I blow out a breath of relief as I park and race up her steps.

"You're missing all the fun," I say through her door when I see her walking through her house with paint all over her— per the usual this past year.

"I heard the beard challenge is over!" she says around a cheer. "Dad swung by to inform me this morning. But your brothers are going to kill you."

I push through the door, joining her as she starts to paint a sculpture, and keep all my inner thoughts about Benson to myself.

I fill her in on the near-ice-tits encounter I had this morning, and she listens and laughs at my expense. I love our friendship.

"I'm not really sure what it means for the town," she says, distracted as she moves an errant curl away from her face to see better, before she dabs some red on the face of her sculpture.

"It means all those 'Fear the Beard' campaign slogans are no longer important," I joke.

She flashes a grin. "It'll be neat to see what the guys actually look like. I haven't seen a face since they hit puberty, for the most part. My dad's beard is so bad that he has to braid it when he's working to keep it out of the machines. And watching the men in this town eat…ew…"

I nod, wondering idly if Benson will lose his beard. And don't announce aloud that I kind of don't want him to.

See? I'm sick or something.

Maybe it's the weather.

I've always been drawn to his voice. Always loved the way he smelled.

But until straddling him all night, I never thought about stripping him naked and having my way with him. Okay, so the thought has crossed my mind, but right now it's like it won't leave my mind. And that *is* a first.

"What's on your mind, Lilah Vincent?" she asks, and I sigh.

"Beards."

Chapter 5

Wild Ones Tip #469
You have to be crazy as hell if you think you can hang with the
Wild Ones. It's rare we ever do anything the easy way.

BENSON

Slightly annoyed, I glance out the window again to see
there's still no sign of her before I step into the shower.

Damn Liam. Damn beard challenge. Damn Vincent
brothers.

I woke up wondering if I was fucking dreaming this
morning when she was straddling my dick like it was her job,
all mussed and flushed on top of me. It was so surreal that I
thought there was no way it was actually happening. No way
she ground herself against me like she was in as much pain as
I was.

I almost—*almost*—pulled those little shorts to the side to
show her what she's been missing all this time. It was a
tortured moment of indecision, because shit could have gotten
awkward real damn quick.

Then fucking Bill called.

Damn dead chipmunks and their level of crazy. Lilah's
crazy as hell too, but she's also my crazy girl. She never dates
the cuntwads her aunt brings to her like plated edibles.

She always sticks with me.

Obviously she's mine. Everyone knows it—even Paul who also pissed me off today. Why the actual fuck did she wear that outfit? It was practically see-through.

Okay, that's an exaggeration, but it was very fucking thin, and there wasn't a lot that could be ignored.

Her body was showcased.

Her ass was practically begging to be touched.

Then those signature combat boots of hers just set it all off like a wet dream.

Every guy out there—sans the married and the family—momentarily forgot she was a Wild One and also forgot she was mine.

Guys around here aren't going after the Wild Women.

Crazy, remember?

Plenty of less crazy women are around town and completely single. So the Wild Girls don't usually get that sort of attention, even if some of them are the hottest in town. Most believe the crazy-to-hot scale is tilted too far in the wrong direction.

Personally, I wouldn't be able to be with anyone but Lilah. Life would be too boring.

Groaning, I curse myself. I had my opportunity, and Bill made me piss it away over those damn beards.

Though I might have gotten annoyed with Lilah's complete disinterest in the beard, even I have to admit it had gotten unsanitary. Eating became a chore when you had to tie back half the hair just to get the food to your mouth. A lot of fucking pointless grooming too, considering I never wanted a beard *that* big.

Leaning back into the spray of the shower, I blow out a breath. I really hope she doesn't wear those skimpy shorts around me ever again.

Next time, I may just go through with pulling them to the side and fucking her until she realizes she's been mine for three fucking years, even if neither of us realized it then.

For now, my hand goes to my cock, and I replay this morning out completely differently. My hand moves as I picture Lilah waking up on top of me, grinding just the way she did.

Only this time, no phone rings. I fist a handful of her hair with one hand, and my other hand rips those fucking shorts to the side, giving me a peek at the part of her body I want to touch with every part of my body.

I thrust into her, and she calls out my name, while her nails scrape down my chest.

That's as far as I get before my knees try to buckle and pleasure spikes through my spine. My eyes roll back in my head, and my body grows lax as the hot water washes away yet another Lilah Vincent fantasy.

I hear that loud ass Jeep of her aunt's coming down the road, and a grin curls my lips.

Maybe the fantasy can finally be the real fucking thing.

She can't hide behind my beard any longer.

Chapter **6**

Wild Ones Tip #129
A surprised Wild One is always a wildcard.
Carry a helmet and condom just in case—you never know
which one you'll need.

LILAH

I drive back to Benson's house, warily scouring my surroundings. I keep expecting my brothers to pop out at any minute.

Maybe they're still warming up.

I pull up to his house, still half expecting the two revenge seekers to hop out with scissors and cut my hair off.

When nothing happens, I bang on the back door. Or front door. I'm not really sure which is the back or front, considering the lake is used more in the summer than the roads, in Benson's case.

"Give me a second," I hear Benson calling out from above me. "I just got out of the shower."

Don't think dirty thoughts. Don't think dirty thoughts.

I look up, but I can't see the second floor because of the porch roof.

"Why'd you lock the doors?" I ask.

"Your brothers."

Ah. Gotcha.

"I was wondering where you went," he calls down.

"Sorry. Figured I'd better grab some clothes before those two thawed and came after me. Then went to town, since I had to drive around. We should have taken two boats this morning."

He grows quiet, and I wonder where he is, until the door suddenly swings open in front of me, and three things happen at once.

My mouth dries.

My heart tries to kick out of my chest.

My entire body takes notice of the fact I'm definitely a woman.

I eye the man before me, taking in the towel on his bare shoulder. My gaze shamelessly rakes over all the contours and outlines of the hard body he's been hiding away.

Abs. Benson Nolans has abs. Six of them, to be exact.

Those fancy sweats are hanging off his hips, revealing the all-too-mouthwatering V that disappears behind the waistband, teasing me with what lies at the end.

My eyes snap up, and that's when I see a man too sexy to be natural. Benson Nolans has a face my vagina wants to get to know.

Gone is the wiry, unkempt, bushy beard. In its place is an intentional, trimmed and neat beard that outlines a strong, masculine jaw. His nose even looks sexier.

His light tan is a little warped, but I'm totally able to overlook that, because...*dayum*.

His lips etch up in a smirk—and panties all over Tomahawk explode in the distance. I never realized how expressive and cocky this man is. Because it's all been hidden under a mound of hair.

Slowly, I take a step back, glance around at all my surroundings, then look back at him as he arches a questioning eyebrow at me. Even that is easier to see, because he apparently got a nice new haircut too.

"Benson?" I ask, confused, hoping it's not really him.

Because I'm in a lot of trouble if it is.

His smile forms, and yeah; I struggle to breathe. Why would you ever cover up that smile?

"I can't possibly look that different," he says, though he has to know he's full of shit.

His hair is shorter — sexier. Even though it's messy, it looks intentionally messy, and I really want to run my fingers through those dark strands.

"Oh yeah. You can look a lot different."

Those same chocolate eyes as always are staring at me, and his voice is still as velvety smooth as ever. I once thought that maybe he was a phone sex operator and that's why he keeps his money-earning ways a secret.

"You coming in or staring at me all night."

Normally I'd make a smartass reply. Tonight? I blush.

I hate this new turn of events. Maybe I shouldn't have gotten rid of the beards, because my life is now officially complicated.

Benson isn't a hit-and-run type of guy. No, I don't do that often. In fact, I've been with a total of four men. Some of those guys were *almost* boyfriends.

Benson locks the door behind him, and he walks in front of me when my feet hesitate to move. I practically drool over his back that is just as sexy as his front.

"You want to watch a movie or something?" he asks. "I need to run back over to your aunt's house to help with the fireworks before tonight."

"Before tonight?" I ask, my eyes watching him as he tosses that towel to a basket near the fridge—total bachelor's house.

"Yeah. Beard challenge is over, and there're going to be fireworks on the lake tonight to represent a new era. Your aunt's words."

I grin, but I'm still staring at his body instead of his face. Finally, my eyes come up just as he turns his head.

"I don't want to stay here without you, since…brothers. I'll drive over there to drop off the Jeep. Then ride back with you in the boat."

He frowns like he's thinking that over. His eyes drop to my jean shorts and my combat boots. What? Combat boots go with everything, and I don't care what anyone says.

The frayed shorts are my sexiest pair, but I usually don't wear them because they're really short. Again, I don't want to question my motives here, but I'm starting to see a very suspicious pattern.

"Ride with me. We'll take the Jeep back tomorrow," he says as his eyes come back up. Then a smile forms. "You finally get your wish. The bad beards are gone."

Yeah, and now I worry what I've done to myself.

"Paul asked me out," I tell him, gauging his reaction closely.

He just arches an eyebrow.

"And?"

Okay, so no jealous outburst. Not that I was expecting one.

"Just found that odd."

Now *I* definitely sound suspicious.

He grins. "If you dated Paul, I'd have to question your sanity. And he's in a hurry to get married, so that wouldn't help your 'settle down without settling down' plan."

My eyebrows go up.

"What?"

"You didn't want to date Liam because you thought he wouldn't settle down. Then you turned around and said you didn't want to settle down. Can't help but wonder if you just don't want anyone at all right now."

That's not true. But at least that means he hasn't noticed me raking my eyes over him in a constant scandalous appraisal lately.

"I don't want to be treated like another notch by someone I have to see regularly, but I also don't want a serious relationship."

He shrugs while looking away. "Why's that?" he asks, sounding casual as he picks up a shirt and tugs it over his head, covering up that secretly perfect body.

"Because of the pressure."

He turns to face me, his eyebrows going up in confusion. "Pressure?"

"It's Tomahawk," I groan. "You get a boyfriend, people start constantly asking when you're getting married. You get married, people bombard you with questions about when you're going to conceive. You pop out a baby, people want to know when the next one is coming out of you." I take a deep breath. "Pressure."

He laughs outright, and I narrow my eyes at him. It's easier to remember this is Benson when he's laughing at me.

"So you don't want to date anyone, because of peer pressure to have babies?"

"And to get married," I remind him. "But yeah, also the baby fear. My mother and Aunt Penny were twins. Fraternal twins, but still twins. I'm one-third of a set of Triplets."

He looks adorably confused. I love being able to read his expressive, sexy, very distracting face.

"Triplets, Benson," I repeat. "My family is known for popping out multiples at one time. I'm not ready for one kid, much less multiples."

He grins broader. "It's funny how you think it's anyone's decision other than yours. Just tell people to leave you alone."

"You need to remember that you haven't dated anyone from here. Trust me. The pressure gets to you. I broke up with my ninth grade boyfriend—"

"Who?" he interrupts, brow creasing.

"Tim—"

"Tim Forrester?" he asks incredulously.

"He was hot in ninth grade. Pre-beard."

He just looks at me like I'm crazy. "Did you have sex with him?

I make a sour face. "Ew. No. I didn't have sex until I was seventeen and living in Seattle."

He shakes his head, looking away, acting like he doesn't want to hear that part. It's totally an overshare, so I get it.

"Anyway, I broke up with him because his mother was constantly asking when we were getting married. It was shortly after I lost my parents—*can you say insensitive, by the way?* Best decision I ever made, because Tim was married the day Rebecca turned eighteen."

His lips purse, his eyes on me again. "Not everyone has parents living here. Not all mothers would pressure you like that."

"Aunt. Penny."

His smile cracks on that one. "Touché."

"So are we going or not?"

"You wearing that?" he asks, his hand gesturing to my shorts.

"It's summer."

"Still gets cool at night in the summer," he says, eyeing me.

He's right, but I'm committed to showing some leg right now. There's a reason I borrowed Kylie's shower to shave my legs before I left her place.

He seemed fascinated with them earlier, and I did get that weird date request from Paul — who is terrified of my brothers and doesn't particularly like me. All from a little extra leg.

My hair is fixed now, since my shower. I even donned a little makeup. Not that he's seemed to notice. *Annnnd* I'm back to feeling self-conscious. Not cool.

Maybe he should grow that beard back until I know how I feel about whatever he's doing to me.

"You coming?" he asks.

Loaded question.

Usually, I skip right up to him, not the least bit intimidated. But now…totally intimidated.

He leads me out the lake-facing door, and I swallow as he tosses his arm around my shoulders before locking his door. He's put his arm around me a thousand times. Never once has it felt like more than a friendly gesture.

His intentions are still friendly, but mine seem to be the ones obscured.

"So the face is better than the beard?" he asks, smiling down at me.

My knees actually go weak. Not kidding. It's humiliating when I almost fall.

Benson quickly steadies me, looking around for a reason as to why I was seconds away from slamming head-first into the ground. "Ankle turned," I lie, and he frowns as he looks back down at me.

"You hurt?"

I shake my head. "Just happens. No biggie."

He nods, accepting the lie, and he guides me down the dock. My tee has a 'Fear the Beard' logo on it, just to really rub it in. Benson seems to notice it for the first time, laughing as he hops into the boat and helps me down.

"Of course that's what you'd wear," he says, smiling like it's a good thing.

I try to ignore the way it feels when he grabs my waist this time, but I can't. I shudder in his grip, but he doesn't seem to notice. In fact, I think he's blissfully unaware of my current status.

That's *utter hot mess* status, in case you're wondering.

He pulls us away, and he drives the distance across the lake to my aunt's house. I'm all too happy to let him help me out, and he follows behind me.

My aunt walks out with a tray of cupcakes in her hands, beaming when she sees me. But when her eyes go over my shoulder to Benson, she drops the tray of cupcakes.

"Benson?" she gasps.

The cupcakes turn into ant food when they tumble around on the grass, and Benson smirks as he runs a nervous hand over the back of his neck.

"I can't possibly look that different," he grumbles.

"Oh yes. Oh, yes, you can," she says while fanning herself with her hand.

The mosquitos will be out soon, so I walk off, abandoning them as I grab the unscented spray that works the best on me and spritz down. I notice my brothers glaring at me, and I smile wickedly at them.

My uncle would kill them if they touched me in front of him.

I even twirl my hair around my finger like an evil, glass-eyed dolly for good measure. Just wait until my next act of revenge on them. It'll give me a reason to stay at Benson's longer.

"You're hiding from us," Killian states flatly when he's right in front of me.

"You idiots still need to fix my dock. And my bed. And I want my ceiling fan back too."

"You cut off our beards, and you think we still owe you?" Hale asks, his eyes wide as he joins us. "You're insane! My balls are still quivering."

Their faces are clean shaven. I almost forgot what they looked like after all these years.

Two arms come around my waist, and I resist the urge to sigh as I lean back on Benson. My brothers glance at the contact, and as one, both their eyes narrow and settle on the man behind me.

"Everything okay over here?" Benson asks.

"You're touching our sister," Killian accuses.

"I've touched your sister numerous times before," he points out.

"Yeah, but you didn't look like you do now, barely bearded and all. And she didn't get that dreamy look on her face before either," Hale says calmly, but there's an edge to his tone.

Apparently, Benson without a bushy beard is less scary to my brothers than Benson with a bushy beard. I can sort of understand that. Doesn't make it suck less in this moment.

I actually feel the blush as it races over my body, and start praying it turns dark in two seconds, even though it's still at least two or three hours until sunset.

"Dreamy look, huh?" Benson asks, sounding amused.

I refuse to turn and look at him. Instead, I give the death glare to my idiot brothers. Neither of them even glance at me to see it though, and they all stand a head over me, making it impossible to put my face in their line of vision even with the help of my tiptoes — that I'm pointlessly using. Short girl problems.

"What the hell is going on in your house?" Killian demands. "I thought you two were just friends."

"We are," Benson drawls, but he moves a little closer.

I practically feel the mockery in his tone.

"She's our only sister," they remind him.

"I'm aware."

See? The few times I've considered dating, this has happened. It's always mortifying and it usually terrifies any guy who even toys with the idea seeing me more than once.

"We don't like guys who touch our sister," Hale goes on, standing to his full, very tall height.

"You two are welcome to remove my hands from her," Benson taunts.

They eye him, eye me, then eye where his hands rest across my middle. I bet they think of his spinning kick thingy, because I don't see them lunging yet.

"We'll be watching you," Killian warns, pointing a finger at Benson before he moves to where the beer is resting in an ice chest.

I blow out a long breath, and Benson laughs behind me. "All these years I've had my hands on you, but I lose a chunk of my beard, so *now* they're threatening me."

I try to play it off, shrugging. "I'm surprised they haven't threatened you sooner."

I turn around, hoping I'm not fifty shades of red, and he grins down at me.

"Because I touch you?" he asks.

"And because I crash at your place from time to time," I add, pressing against him a little more.

His eyes lock on mine, and I take in every beautiful inch of his face, admiring how much better it is to be this close without having a beard tickling me.

"Benson, did you bring them?" my uncle asks, interrupting our moment.

My eyes almost pop out of my head. Uncle Bill's beard is still there, but it's neatly trimmed, much shorter, and you can see his mouth now.

"See? He knew who I was," Benson says, cocking an eyebrow at me.

"Actually," Uncle Bill says, clearing his throat and grinning sheepishly. "I had to get Penny to help me find you. Didn't realize that was you."

Benson's eyebrows go up, and I grin triumphantly as they walk off to do whatever.

"If he hurts you, you realize we'll have to break both his legs." Killian's voice startles me, since I had no idea he was anywhere around.

Hale hands me a beer that I inspect with dubious caution before opening.

"Possibly an arm or two as well," Hale adds.

"It's not like that," I say on a sigh before sipping the beer.

My eyes linger on Benson as he smiles and says something to my uncle.

"If you say so," Killian murmurs.

"We'll get your bed fixed tomorrow so you can get back to your cabin," Hale says adamantly.

"That's not the only reason I'm avoiding my cabin," I say, narrowing my eyes. "I know you're planning something terrible to punish me for the beard debacle."

"We were." Killian nods as he says this. "But that was before we realized how cozy you are with Benson. We'll call a truce, and you can come home."

"I don't believe you."

They exchange a look, then return their gazes to me.

"Seriously. Get home. We'll call a truce on the graves."

I swallow hard. They're serious.

"All this over Benson? We've been friends for years. I've spent the night at his house before."

"But he looks like a dude you'd want now. So get home."

With that, they turn and walk away, and I flip them off to their backs as I roll my eyes and smile to myself.

"Well, I'll be damned," Aunt Penny says, looking out as a bunch of boats full of women cruise this way.

That's more than twenty. When did we get more than twenty single women? Why was I not informed of this very crucial development at a time like this?

"Looks like the beardless party is bringing the women back," she goes on.

It's apparently also bringing in women I didn't even know existed.

Howls and whistles sound out as beardless, or mostly beardless, men welcome the incoming hordes of women, and I sit back, watching as several start talking to Benson.

Uh-oh.

Chapter 7

Wild Ones Tip #72
Know the brand of crazy you're dealing with.
It could save your balls. Or your vagina lips.

LILAH

I'm four beers in when I consider smashing Lindy's face in with the empty bottles beside me or cutting off her vagina lips with the broken glass.

For the past three years, at these little gatherings, I was one of maybe three women here. The women didn't want to come to these things, and Aunt Penny made me attend.

Hell, not even Delaney would come, even when I begged her, because she found it boring. Oh, but she's here tonight.

My brothers were banned pretty often from Aunt Penny's events, which put me on my own. Over those years, Benson and I became friends, and it was an unspoken arrangement that we'd hang out together to endure these things as a team.

Now Benson is drinking with Paul—who I didn't recognize without his bushy red beard—while Lindy Perkins stands right up against him like I usually do. I never realized before today how much we touch.

But now that I see another woman touching him, I can't help but feel territorial.

And I have no right.

Usually he's shy and quiet. Or just quiet. Not tonight. His confidence is buzzing. It's a really good look on him.

I just assumed he'd still be the same Benson even with an extra shot of confidence.

Benson looks up, catching me looking at him, and I cut my gaze away just as Liam walks toward me, a smile playing on his lips.

"There's a face I recognize," he says in relief. "With all these beards gone, I feel like I have to meet everyone all over again."

I force a smile as he takes the empty seat next to me. I turn my body to fully face him, straddling the picnic table bench, so that I can no longer see Lindy touching Benson. The way I'm usually touching him.

Because they're not friends and we are.

Time for a new friend, it seems. Benson wants to be shared, and I can't stand the gnawing, unprecedented jealousy I'm fighting.

I'm being ridiculous. I can't stop being his friend even if he does get a girlfriend. I'll just have to make her life hell — simple task for a girl like me — until she's gone.

There. Plan made. Problem solved.

"Are you relieved you're no longer the only eligible bachelor in Tomahawk?" I muse.

His grin grows. "Yeah. Very. I'm not big on a lot of attention. Didn't expect that in a town so small."

"It'll calm down now, and we'll be a normal bunch before you know it."

As if summoned by that promise, there's suddenly a shrill squeal, and one of my brothers is soaring through the air over our heads, his feet running on air. Hale lands in the lake so hard the water splashes straight up like a cannon just fired from beneath it.

I turn to see the rubber bungie mess behind me that just launched him.

"You idiots griped about that water, and you build *that*?" I ask, gesturing to the ludicrous contraption that looks like they stole parts of a trampoline to assemble that thing.

Killian grins at me, as Hale hoots from the water, climbing out.

"Couldn't resist. Always wanted to try this!" Hale adds.

I shake my head, and I look back over to Liam to find him laughing. "Yeah. Terribly boring."

"Well, my brothers don't count. They have a tendency to be anything but boring. But it usually drives you insane instead of making you laugh. Just wait until they let bugs invade your panties."

It's not boring at all in Tomahawk when you live close to a corner of Wild Ones, but I don't bother telling him that. He's still new.

His eyebrows go up at the panty remark, and I laugh to myself while shaking my head.

Hale drops another beer off in my hand as he drips cool water everywhere on his way by, and I watch him suspiciously.

"What's that look for?" Liam asks, curious.

"He's trying to get me drunk. Which makes me worry about the reasons as to why. Last time they got me drunk, I ended up in a canoe and woke up all the way around the double bend of the lake. My arms felt like they were going to fall off by the time I managed to paddle home."

He snorts, shaking his head as laughter creeps out.

"I thought your aunt said she didn't allow them over here," he says through his chuckles.

"Beardless night is apparently the exception. I'm sure she'll regret that before the night is over."

"Gotcha. So a canoe, huh?" he asks, apparently wanting me to continue.

"That canoe trip took me past two of the other three corners, and I got shot with paintballs when I passed the Malone corner."

"This odd shaped lake has only four corners?" he asks.

"Metaphorical corners. Four of them. There are probably really like forty literal corners. The wildest of the Wild Ones—
"

"Wild Ones?" he asks, sitting up straighter, suddenly very interested.

I'm not sure why that rouses his interest so much, but I'm tipsy enough to continue running my mouth about Tomahawk's system of crazy. Liam is growing on me, since he seems genuine and nice enough.

"Yes. The Wild Ones are put on very different parts of the lake to help break up some of the crazy. Vincents—my brothers and I—are on this end. Malones are on another 'corner,' Nickels are on another, and the final are the Wilders."

"Wilders? You're serious?" he asks incredulously.

I nod. "True to their name, they're even worse than us, and that's saying a lot, because…have you met my brothers?"

He laughs to himself. "I had no idea there was a political system on who was the wildest."

"Yep. And the crazy scale is often adjusting to accommodate us all. My dad moved out here when he was younger, and raised the Vincent name up to full-blown heathen status with my mother at his side. My brothers and I have carried on the tradition. My aunt and uncle are only guilty by association."

"So you've always lived here?"

I nod. "Mostly. Other than the one year of graphic design school. I don't have a degree, but I learned all I needed to get my business started, and I make good money. Online, that is. Not so much here."

"Doing what?" he asks, genuinely interested.

"Book cover design. Website design. Logo design. Anything in need of a graphic designer really."

He flashes that smile again.

"And what about your parents?"

I go a little still, then recover quickly. "They died in a car accident when I was fifteen," I say, clearing my throat. His face is instantly coated in remorse. "They were going to drive down to Seattle for their anniversary. Black ice on the road caught them by surprise. But at least they had each other when they died. One could have never survived without the other."

He blows out a long, regretful breath.

"I'm sorry. I didn't know."

"We moved on. It's fine. You're not dredging up memories I can't face. We've faced all of it head on with Aunt Penny and Uncle Bill. I'm just not used to someone not knowing the story."

I glance over my shoulder to see Delaney is now talking to Benson, even though he looks less chipper now than he did before. His eyes are on me, and I offer a tight smile.

Delaney would back off immediately if I said something, but why bother? If Benson wants to have fun with other women and ignore me — the girl who has been hanging with him, beard and all, for the past few years — then he's allowed to do that.

I refocus my attention on Liam as he leans back, running a hand through his blond hair.

"You said Malones were one of these wild families?" he asks.

"Yeah. You've heard of them?"

He shrugs, a small, secretive smile tugging at his lips. "Maybe. Are you enemies or something?"

"No. No Wild Ones are enemies to each other. It's not like that. My best girl friend is a Malone. Her dad and cousins like to shoot us with paintballs when they spot us on the water, because my brothers accidentally blew up their dock last summer."

He chokes on his beer. "How do you *accidentally* blow up a dock?"

"Pipe bomb. They were trying to blow a big stump out of the water, but Hale tripped, and the bomb flew out of his hand. It caught the edge of the dock just as it went off. No one was hurt, but they still hold a silly grudge."

He laughs harder, as though he's not believing this. It's a true story. Not even one of the most unbelievable either.

"They rebuilt the dock to be even better than it was, but a Vincent still gets shot with a paintball if they get anywhere near that dock now."

"Damn," he says on a chuckle, then looks around and takes a deep breath, silence falling over us comfortably.

"Never was able to just relax like this in LA. I almost moved to Seattle for a while," he finally says.

"What changed your mind?" I ask.

"The rain," he answers without hesitation, to which I laugh.

"The rain can be fierce here, too. We've just got a small, semi-dry spell before it starts back up near the end of summer."

He nods, still smiling as he stares out at the lake. More boats are moving this way, but despite the small disturbance, it's still peaceful.

"I'm okay with the rain now," he says softly.

"Why's that?" I ask, leaning up on the picnic table and bracing my head with my hand.

"The rain forces me to slow down, and now I actually want to slow down. Life has a way of changing you. And I finally realized one day that I had no real friends, my job was controlling my life, I was moving at the speed of light, yet staying in the same stagnant spot, and my money brought about some of the worst of humanity disguised as the best. The biggest eye-opener was when I got hurt in a sky-diving accident, and barely managed to walk away with my life. Saved by pure dumb luck and one crazy girl."

"What?" I ask, genuinely interested.

"The parachute malfunctioned and opened late. I still managed to slow my speed enough to land a little softer, and also had enough time to steer myself over water. I was banged up and suffered a broken leg instead of dying. A girl diving with us that day pulled me out before I could drown."

My heart is actually racing as he turns to face me again.

"My family didn't call to check on me. My so-called friends didn't bother stopping by or calling, other than the few who feigned concern. Everything fun suddenly seemed so empty, because I realized no one really cared about me. Only one girl acted like she truly gave a damn, and I barely even knew her."

"What was her name?"

He flashes me a grin.

"I'll tell you soon. She's actually the reason I decided to buy the cabin out here. This is her hometown."

My jaw drops, and he winks at me.

"So that explains the total lack of interest in all things with a vagina. I sort of wondered if you were into men," I say thoughtfully.

He barks out a laugh, and I smile as he shakes his head. "Nah. I'm still working up the courage to tell her I stalked her here. I haven't seen her out yet, but in a place this small, it's bound to happen sooner or later. I just didn't expect everyone to be so spread out."

I start to try to pry a name out of him again, when suddenly he's smiling at something over my shoulder. "Hey, I'm Liam Harper."

"I know. We've met multiple times now," Benson says, his body moving in behind me on my seat at the picnic table.

His legs come up beside mine as he straddles the seat and me from behind. His hands rest on his legs, but just his proximity is having me swallow harder.

Liam looks confused for the barest second before his eyebrows hit his hairline. "Benson Nolans?"

"Oh, for fuck's sake. I don't look that different," Benson groans.

"Yeah. Yeah, you do," Liam says, and I tilt my head back on Benson's chest to smile up at him.

He glares down at me, but his twitching lips betray him. Without thinking, I reach up, my fingers touching the side of his face. He goes stiff behind me, the humor in his eyes dying.

"I like being able to finally see a damn expression," I tell him, even though I'm saying this upside down.

His smile returns as my fingers trace down the surprisingly soft remnants of his beard. It's not wiry anymore; short like this, it feels like silk. Okay, not that soft, but definitely soft enough to feel inviting.

"Benson!" Delaney calls, then stops when she sees us.

She deflates almost instantly, and actually looks hurt for a brief second. I'll explain to her later that Benson has been mine for three years, but I didn't realize it until I woke up on top of him.

"Do not leave me alone with them," Benson says quietly as I lower my hand, and I hear Liam start to laugh.

"Glad I came in at the end of this beard thing," Liam says, causing Benson's lips to twitch.

"You're the one who was over there with them. I always hang out in this exact spot," I point out, still looking up at Benson, who frowns down at me.

"I had to talk to Paul about importing some materials too big to drive on that rickety road behind my place. He's the one with the barge. Then I had to listen to fifteen stories about random things before I could get away from him. You know how Paul is."

And now I feel like I've been pouting for no reason.

I shrug, looking back over at Liam, who is staring at anything but us right now as he leans back on the picnic table.

Benson wouldn't embarrass someone by shrugging them off, hence the reason Lindy and Delaney touching him didn't get rebuffed. I still don't like it. I'd rather him be an ass. I'm used to my brothers — they'd both be total assholes.

"I kind of miss my beard right now," Benson grumbles when Lindy starts walking our way.

"I miss your beard too," I say too quietly for him to hear.

No other women noticed him before I stupidly helped get that bad beard gone. Now it feels like I'm struggling to keep him to myself like I've done for the past three years.

"Lindy!" Aunt Penny yells before Lindy can reach us. "I need help with these desserts!"

Lindy stares at Benson for a beat, but he leans over like he's hiding beside my face, his breath tickling my neck until I laugh, unable to stop it. His arms are strong around my waist as they tighten there.

I've never once gotten a death glare from another woman.

Not a damn one.

Until now.

I never should have ruined the beards.

"Coming," Lindy says before spinning on a heel. "Maybe Lilah could help us too," she adds so sweetly.

"Lilah always helps. She's at all these gatherings. Thought maybe some of you new girls could pull your weight for the night," Aunt Penny, the most awesome woman in the universe, says.

Benson snickers beside me as I laugh, and Liam even chuckles.

His eyes scan the place, and I secretly wonder who's missing. It's a small town. Sure, there are more single women than I realized initially, but I don't know who he'd be looking for.

"Still don't see her?" I ask.

He shakes his head, darting an apprehensive glance to Benson, and I realize he doesn't want him knowing.

Got it.

"See who?" Benson asks.

"One of the girls here asked him for a three-way. He's trying to avoid her," I deadpan.

Liam's lips twitch when Benson strangles on air, and I wink at him, letting him know I'm damn good at keeping secrets.

"I don't want to stick around for fireworks. Think they'd get mad if we bailed early? All the buzz over my beard being gone is getting annoying," Benson says close to my ear.

Butterflies. I've totally got butterflies. Because I'm fairly sure he's telling me I'm coming with him, or at least assuming I am.

That's normal, but tonight it seems a little different. I think. Or maybe I'm being a girl and seeing something that's not there.

"Sure," I say all too readily.

He stands, his arm sliding around my waist, and we both tell Liam *bye* before making our way toward the boat.

"Hey, Nolans. We need to talk to you," Killian says, eyeing the hand Benson has on my waist.

Benson sighs. "Ignore them," I tell him.

"Can't. Just let me deal with it, then we'll get out of here."

Even though I try to stop him, he still goes to my brothers, who smirk at me. Fortunately, I've seen Benson rough both of them up in the past. Like that time they broke my bathroom window and I got stung by a bunch of bees as a result. Did I mention they broke my window with a limb that had a beehive on it?

Yeah. They were like Pooh Bear going for honey, and it didn't end well for me when the limb *and* hive crashed through my bathroom window as I was showering.

The damn hive didn't have any honey in it. It wasn't honey bees.

Dick bags.

I know they had to know that.

Benson literally beat the shit out of them for a while before he made them go buy me comfort foods, hydrocortisone cream, and various other things while he patched up a temporary window and ordered me a new one.

That *they* paid for.

Why didn't I think I liked him sooner?

I really should have just slept on top of his chest a year or two ago. Then I could have had him before he lost the beard and every other girl wanted him.

"So what's up with that?" Delaney asks me, her tone guarded as she stares at Benson talking to my brothers.

He's smirking. They're not smiling at all.

"What's up with what?" I ask as I turn to face her, playing dumb.

She narrows her eyes at me. "You've never acted interested in anyone, then I flirt half the day with him, competing with Lindy this entire time, and suddenly you're cuddled up with him on the picnic table? Seriously, what gives?"

My smile slowly spreads. "You never saw him before he lost the bad beard, did you?"

She frowns. "What?"

"Delaney, that is maybe a little more affectionate than we've been in the past, but not much. We're always touching, and always hanging out at these gatherings—not that you're here to see that. I do his shopping on Tuesdays when I go into town. Benson and I have been friends for three years at least. I've even talked about him to you, and it's like you never paid attention when I said his name. Nothing romantically related, but he came up in many conversations."

Her entire face falls. "Oh," she says, her face reddening.

The sun is starting to set now, and she fidgets awkwardly, focusing on where the massive ball of fire is sinking into the horizon.

"Makes sense why he was so uncomfortable with us. I thought it was just because he was shy and not used to the attention. Found it sort of cute or endearing. Now I feel stupid."

I laugh lightly. "No need. I feel stupid for making the beards go away."

Her eyes widen and she grabs my shoulders, shaking me a little. There's my Delaney. "Don't you *ever* say that again. This town finally, *finally* has men in it that don't look like they crawled out of a gutter or survived an island where no one had to look at them for a decade. We should erect a statue of you to commemorate this momentous occasion that has forever changed Tomahawk for the better."

We both dissolve into laughter, and Benson is suddenly back, his arm slipping around my waist and dragging me closer.

"What'd I miss?" he asks, though he feels a little stiff.

Delaney's eyes twinkle with humor, and she winks at me. "Nothing. Just talking about sculptures. I'm going to go keep Paul company."

She saunters away, and Benson relaxes against me. "Let's go before someone else tries to stop us."

"What'd my brothers say?" I ask as he pulls my hand.

"Threatened me with bodily harm if I took your virginity."

I stumble over my own feet, and he laughs, turning to face me.

"I'm not a virgin," I quickly tell him.

"I don't think they want to accept that as the truth."

I glare over my shoulder at my two brothers, who are staring at us with their arms crossed over their chests, daring Benson to make a wrong move.

"You can still kick their asses, right?" I ask as Benson tugs me to his boat, helping me off the dock.

"One on one in a fair fight? Definitely."

Chapter 8

Wild Ones Tip #413
If a squirrel has firecrackers, run for your damn life.

Benson brings me another beer, popping the top on one of his own, as he shrugs out of his shirt.

My eyes widen, and I grip the beer in my hand too tightly. He tosses the shirt away, and he sits down beside me, dropping his arm over my shoulders like it's no big deal that he's now shirtless.

And touching me.

And shirtless.

I try to fix my attention on the TV, but it's too hard.

"We'll go out when we hear the fireworks starting," he says. "But all the beer has me burning up."

I can't help myself; I poke his stomach to see if it's as hard as it looks, and he jerks, looking down at me like I'm a crazy girl.

"How are you so hard?"

He chokes on his beer, and I replay those words in my head.

"I mean your body," I amend.

He laughs lightly, shaking his head. "I kayak first thing in the morning almost every morning, which you know. I work on various projects—physically demanding projects, which you know. You've seen my gym; it's not just for looks. Not to mention the running—"

"You run?" I ask, interrupting him as horror washes over me. "On purpose?"

His smile slowly forms. I really like that smile he's been hiding for too long. "Yeah. At least once a day, usually early mornings…why?"

I shudder dramatically. "I don't know you at all."

A rumble of laughter escapes him as I try to process that.

"I don't think we can be friends anymore," I tell him, looking back at the imposter who I thought was awesome just a few seconds ago.

He just grins broader, not taking this as seriously as he should.

"So Liam and you looked chummy tonight," he says, deflecting.

"Well, he didn't confess to something as nasty as running *on purpose*."

That smile only grows. "You trading me in for him as a friend? Or was he finally asking you out?"

I shrug, smirking as I redirect my attention to the TV.

"He's not interested in me in that way. And I'm not interested in him. Too pretty for me."

"Because he doesn't have a beard," he says hesitantly.

"No. Because he's freakishly gorgeous."

He bristles beside me, and I turn to face him.

"Why the inquisition?" I muse, echoing his words from that odd little breakfast we shared.

"Just curious," he says before turning his beer up.

Absently, I notice his other hand is twirling strands of my hair around it.

"Weirdly, I know more about his story before Tomahawk than I know about yours. And we've known each other for six years. Been friends for three years. I've known Liam for a handful of days."

He clears his throat, shifting uneasily. "What do you want to know?"

"The usual," I say, turning to face him, feeling a little eager to get some answers.

Just as he opens his mouth to speak, there's a loud pounding on the door. Cursing, he stands and goes to answer it, but I almost demand he puts a shirt on when people start walking in.

No one else is allowed to see him like this.

See? Crazy girl alert.

But it's okay, because I'm a Vincent. People expect some crazy.

"Benson!" Paul calls. "Care if we watch the fireworks from over here? Her damn brothers are driving us crazy with that bungie launcher they built," Paul says, gesturing toward me.

Then Lindy walks in, her eyes going straight to the half-naked specimen that is mine. Well, he will be.

I've decided that there's no way I can keep living in denial. Time to move on to another phase and hope Benson wants me too. I just don't know how to test those waters without being awkward about it.

Benson has been a permanent fixture in my life for a while, and ever since sleeping on top of him, I haven't been able to get him out of my head. And it's Benson. We're friends. We're best friends, actually.

That could be a good thing, right?

Lindy smiles brightly at him as several other men and women walk in. I don't bother looking at their faces, because I'm too concentrated on Benson as he walks back toward me.

"Looks like I don't have a choice," he tells Paul. "But this better mean my materials get moved up to the top of the list."

Paul nods, grinning with delight, as Delaney drops to his lap on the chair next to us. Lindy moves toward us, but Benson literally pulls me onto his lap before she can make a move.

Again, I get the evil eye, even as I try not to grin.

Lindy is ballsy, but she's not a Vincent or a Wild One. She knows I trump her level of crazy, and I see the moment she knows she can't compete.

Benson's arms go around my waist, and he buries his face in my neck. "Tell me when she's gone," he whispers, and I fight really hard not to laugh.

"Lindy! Come join us," someone shouts from the side.

Benson's pool table is coming in handy as Lindy goes to show off her skills in her daisy dukes.

"Best. Night. Ever," Paul sighs as Delaney smiles against his lips.

Benson shakes his head, his face still against my neck.

"She's gone," I tell him, and he lifts his head, scanning the room to make sure I'm not tricking him.

He doesn't let me out of his lap, so I stay in place as Delaney tells us about what my brothers were doing.

Apparently they decided watermelons were awesome ammo for their new contraption.

They also thought Aunt Penny's pies were awesome ammo.

And I give it maybe fifteen more minutes before she's chasing them with the BB gun until they're off her property.

Benson's hands stay clasped around my middle as I talk to Delaney about my trip out to Seattle that's coming up next month for a graphic design seminar I want to attend. That's when Lindy returns.

"So, you two got cozy quick," Lindy says, her annoyed eyes betraying her smiling lips.

She's carefully navigating, scoping out my crazy reach, testing the waters.

"They're always like that," Paul says dismissively, which has Lindy deflating like Delaney did earlier.

Sheesh. Has no one ever noticed him at all when he was with me? It's like he was invisible or something.

Benson gulps down another beer, and I start noticing that he's getting drunk when his hands start drifting over my body, touching me a little less safely. His thumb even brushes my breast once.

This isn't the first time, but it's the first time I haven't stopped his hands while laughing it off.

Usually he gets drunk, gets handsy, then he's mortified the next day. By *usually*, I mean this has happened a total of five times. It's why he rarely drinks around me.

Tonight, however, I don't bat his hands away.

I also know that I should, because we're both a little tipsy, which is also a first. Usually one stays sober while the other drinks. And by usually, again, like a handful of times.

I've been handsy before on Benson, according to Paul, but I don't remember it, and Aunt Penny never saw it. And Benson said it never happened. So…who knows?

I lean back, sighing as Benson's lips brush my neck. Something he'd never, *ever* do sober. Hence the reason I know he's getting drunker by the beer.

I drink more of mine, and he looks over, gesturing toward Delaney who is ramming her tongue down Paul's throat. Paul is in heaven, but I think he's about to have an accident.

According to rumors, it's been a while for him.

I laugh while standing, noticing Lindy is back at the pool table, no longer watching us.

Thunderous *booms* rattles the sky, causing the house to quake, and Benson smiles down at me as we both grab a fresh beer from the ice bucket one of the others set up, and head outside to watch the fireworks.

He tugs me to him, resting his chin on top of my head as I lean back against him. The fireworks sprinkle across the sky, beautiful and bright, demanding attention.

I'm barely able to notice the others coming out to join us, everyone gushing over the beautiful display. My uncle drives for miles to get the good stuff for these things. He has three closets packed full of just fireworks.

Just as another set burst into the sky, I hear a dog barking like crazy, and screams erupting.

I run in, grab the binoculars off Benson's table, and run back out, looking through them.

"What's going on?" Benson asks.

I realize it's Cooter, my brothers' bloodhound that roams around, when he runs in front of a light. But it's what he's chasing that has my heart pattering.

"Cooter," I say on a groan.

There's a squirrel with a set of firecrackers going off on a long string attached to its tail. Cooter is howling, doing all he can to catch the squirrel and the firecrackers. I can't see what happens when they aren't in front of the light.

Then I screech when I hear a loud squeal from across the lake, and suddenly fireworks are shooting this way.

Benson jerks me down to the ground, and the binoculars fall out of my hand as he covers my body with his.

Fireworks *boom* right above us, debris from the too-close explosives raining down on us and his house. Paul screams and yelps as he falls to the ground and starts scooting his ass across it.

"Ow!" he howls.

Another one almost connects with his back, and Benson presses more of his body on top of me until I'm completely shielded.

"Get down!" Benson shouts to all the idiots who haven't ducked for cover yet.

Another firework blasts right above us, knocking his rain gutter loose as the blindingly bright, white blast leaves dots on my vision.

I blink rapidly.

My ears ache from all the close contact noise.

It grows deadly silent as quickly as things got out of hand, and I peer around, still seeing a few dots, wondering if it's safe.

"Are there more?" Benson calls out loudly.

"No! None that are lit!" my uncle calls back. "I'm going to kill those fucking heathens!"

"I'll help!" Benson yells as he stands and helps drag me to my feet.

Leave it to my brothers to get one night back at my aunt's and ruin the fireworks.

"What happened to the squirrel?" I call out.

"Cooter got him," Uncle Bill answers.

I grimace, but silently hope it was one of the squirrel bastards who has been chewing through my wiring in the attic and making my life hell. Benson tugs me to his side.

"Let's get our drink on, beardless animals!" Paul roars, no longer concerned about his scorched ass as he drags Delaney back into Benson's house.

Benson sighs as we both trudge back in.

Why oh why did I get rid of the beards?

Chapter 9

Wild Ones Tip #227
Never listen to drunk confessions, or you might become an accomplice after the fact.

LILAH

People are crashing on couches and in the spare rooms — including mine, apparently. I don't realize this until I push open the door to see Paul and Delaney kissing on the bed I had the other night.

Sighing, I shut the door, and turn around to see a smirking Benson. "You'll have to double with me tonight. It's not like it'll be the first time we've slept together."

His eyes run over my body, and I try to act like I'm as confident as he is. That night is what really changed everything, sent me on this downward spiral into the rabbit hole.

I move toward his room like I'm not internally shaking like crazy.

"Can I borrow a shirt or something?"

He doesn't respond, but as soon as we walk into his room, he pulls out a drawer and tosses me a shirt. I look around his room, since it's the only one in the house I've never seen before.

It always felt like a personal boundary that I never crossed, even though he's seen my room plenty of times.

I happily accept the shirt, and duck into his bathroom — which is not the same bathroom he went into back when I followed him — and gasp.

Because it's massive.

There's a huge walk-in, tiled shower with two showerheads on each side, and one massive rainfall showerhead right in the middle. The glass doors are pristine, as though he always cleans them.

The floors are…holy shit! The floors are heated!

Towels are neatly rolled inside bamboo shelves off to the side, and then there's a towel warmer built into the wall, glass casing surrounding it.

It's a bathroom wet dream.

"You okay in there?" he calls out.

"No. I'm moving into your bathroom. You'll never get rid of me."

His laughter is soft, because he thinks I'm kidding. I'm already doing the math on how big my bed can be.

I almost sing *Hallelujah* when I see the large, granite countertops with so much space you'd never have to worry about things toppling into the wet sink when you're trying to use them. Plenty of drawers for storage too.

It's…perfect.

"Are you still looking at everything?"

"Never coming out," I tell him as I tug my shirt off and replace it with his, then pull my shorts off.

I fold my clothes neatly and take them back out, and he flashes a grin at me as he looks up from his phone. He's sitting on the bed, looking every bit as tempting as he possibly can, as I place my clothes on his dresser.

"Why don't you have a phone?" he asks me randomly. Three years we've been friends, and he asks this question now of all times?

I shrug. "Why would I have one?"

"Well, for business for one."

He arches an eyebrow.

"Facebook has video calling, regular calling, and text. Email has chat boxes for immediate things. Also, my preferred method of communication with my clients is email, because otherwise, they try to monopolize the hours that I carve out for just me. Phones just mean less face-to-face interaction. I prefer to speak to my friends or family in person."

He smiles like he likes that answer. "But sometimes someone might want to call you to tell you to come see them."

"If they want to see me, they know where I live or the other few places to find me. Like all the other Wild Ones, I raise the flag when I'm at the cabin; I put it down when I'm not."

He laughs under his breath. "You're a complicated woman, Lilah Vincent."

"Actually, I'm very uncomplicated. As simple as they come."

His grin turns thoughtful as I near him, and I move onto the bed next to him, careful not to let the shirt ride up.

"That's probably the most wrong I've ever heard you," he finally says.

I snort derisively, stabbing my legs under the covers. I always get cold right before I go to sleep.

Benson shifts, tugging the covers down, and I turn away, trying not to hyperventilate when he takes off his pants, revealing his nice, black boxers. He slides into bed, staggering a little, and his hands immediately go for me, grappling me and pulling me back to him.

"You haven't pushed my hands away tonight. Is it because I finally got rid of the beard?" he muses, his hands sliding down my hip, hesitating where the T-shirt stops.

"No," I say, swallowing thickly.

He presses a kiss to my neck before curving his body around mine a little better. I stare at the wall in front of me like it's fascinating.

"Then why?" he asks quietly.

I shudder when he starts pushing the T-shirt up.

"Because when I woke up on top of you, I realized I wanted to do more than just sleep there."

He groans when his hand slides up my bare hip.

"Are you really not wearing any underwear?" he asks, sounding somewhat tortured.

I swallow audibly this time. "Bugs."

His hand pauses, and then he laughs into the crook of my neck.

"Bugs," he says on a sigh. "Forgot about that."

I turn in his arms, and all the humor leaves his face as my eyes take in his features, studying him now that I can see his expressions so easily.

"What are we doing right now?"

He slides his hand back over me, then he jerks me toward him until our bodies are pressed together completely. My leg comes up over his hip, and I suck in a breath when I feel something really hard and promising right up against my pubic bone.

"I don't really know. But I know I've wanted to do it for the past year."

"The past year?"

He nods slowly, his eyes scanning my face. "Always thought you were gorgeous—maybe even *freakishly gorgeous,*" he says, mocking my last words about Liam. Do I detect a hint of jealousy?

A smile slithers over my lips.

"But at first I thought you weren't the type to stick around here. You'd already gone to Seattle once, so I distanced myself. Then as the years whittled on, I started seeing you as the girl next door, sort of. A constant Vincent nuisance, yet also a breath of fresh air. But never thought of anything more. Then, somehow, we became friends, and I couldn't believe I'd ever *not* been friends with you."

I inch closer to him, and he flicks his gaze over my face again.

"Then one year ago almost exactly, I was burying that damn cat your aunt had saddled me with. I didn't even realize I liked the damn thing until I found it dead at the edge of the lake. You showed up to borrow my axe, but saw what was going on. You never mentioned the fact I was crying like a pussy over a cat, and you helped me bury him. Then you held my hand, said a prayer for him, and stayed the rest of the night while I got drunk and touched you a little inappropriately."

I cock my head.

"You were trying to put moves on me? That wasn't just drunken bullshit?"

He laughs, his eyes lowering briefly. "Pretty much. Never knew it was an issue with the beard."

"The beard was just very distracting. Sleeping on you, feeling that boundary crossed, and waking up feeling unsatisfied…that's when I realized…I still don't know what we're doing," I say on a long sigh.

He grins, staring at me. "Nothing while we've been drinking."

That…irks me. We're supposed to sleep in the same bed and do nothing? Again?!

Okay, so last time it was a couch, but still.

"You're serious?"

His grin only grows. "Yeah. I'm serious. I've waited a year. I can wait one more day to make sure you're sober."

"Why didn't you say anything?"

He shrugs. "You kept saying you weren't ready to settle down. But then there was a little hope when you said Liam wouldn't settle down, almost as though you'd slipped up and said it, then tried to back pedal."

He bends, his delicious breath bathing my lips, and my whole body tenses and burns as a powerful ache forms between my thighs.

"That was when I decided you were ready, because I knew once I had you, I wouldn't be able to give you up. And I won't share."

I lean forward, ready to see if those lips of his are as soft as they look, but he reels back, grinning at me when my eyes open.

"Tomorrow," he says softly.

Lucky for him, I happen to be exhausted tonight.

Chapter **10**

Wild Ones Tip #645
Mean what you say. Or keep your mouth shut. And don't get upset when we put words in your mouth if you plead silence.

LILAH

I jerk awake, feeling around for Benson, but his side of the bed is cold. I do hear muffled words coming from the bathroom, and I stand to go listen.

"I'm sure it'll be fine, Mom. I'm not concerned with any of that. Haven't been in a long time. That's not why I still live here." He grows quiet, and my brow furrows. This is the first time I've ever heard him talk to any of his family.

"Yeah. Two weeks from now. I'll see you guys then."

Again he grows quiet, and I shamelessly press my ear to the door.

"I've already told you I don't care if they come, but it's up to you which rooms they take. They've come plenty of other times. Just so long as it's nowhere near mine, I've never given a damn which rooms they're in."

He groans like he's frustrated.

"I know they're divorced. I don't see her like that anymore. But stop thinking we're going to be that kind of family that doesn't have scars."

I frown, pulling back from the door.

"Look, I have to go. I have some friends who crashed here last night."

Yes, I keep listening, wondering if he might mention me to his mother. Then realize how creepy that sounds and hope he doesn't mention me.

"Yes, I have friends, Mom," he says, sounding amused. "Many of them."

Another beat passes.

"Because it's Tomahawk."

I roll my eyes, inwardly groaning as he chuckles, and I back away from the door. Apparently his family and his friends get the same reasoning as to why one can't know about the other.

I jog back to the bed, looking guilty as hell when he swings open that door. His eyes widen in surprise that I'm awake. Or maybe he's surprised that I'm here. I suddenly feel underdressed, because this is *not* how I envisioned this morning going after last night.

He opens his mouth to speak, when we hear laughter float up the stairs.

"Benson! You awake yet? We can't get your fancy stove to work!" Paul yells. "And we're starving."

He groans, and I tug at the ends of his shirt to cover me a little better.

My boat and Aunt Penny's Jeep are both here, and I decide on the Jeep as he hustles out without saying a word. He's always embarrassed the day after drinking, and last night...things got real.

Now he's dodging me.

Got it. I don't need a sign.

I *do* need pants.

Quickly, I hurry to the room where my clothes are, find something to wear, brush my teeth, and creep down the stairs to the sounds of people chuckling.

"That damn dog destroyed the fireworks," I hear Joey saying. I forgot he was even here last night. There were a lot of people still here when we went to bed.

Sounds like they still are, but I tiptoe out the back—or front!—door to the Jeep. I'm silent as I close the door, and then I crank it and put it in gear, getting out like it's the walk of shame, minus the fun, *shameful* part.

I make the long drive through town, then drive all the way to Aunt Penny's, park her Jeep, and hop out, pulling my backpack on as I go. I slowly walk through the woods, hoping that cougar isn't lurking for round two, since I'm unarmed. Again.

My eyes stay on the bank, somewhat hoping to hear the roar of Benson's boat. But that doesn't happen. And when I get to my cabin, my dock is empty, except for my brothers' boat that is tied off next to the broken end of the dock they still haven't repaired.

I stalk up my steps, into my cabin, and crash to my very uncomfortable couch as I stare up at the ceiling. At least I have work that needs to be done.

I glance into my bedroom, and I grin when I see my brothers really did rebuild my bed to the proper size. It's even made.

I go to the bed, sigh as I pull the covers back and find fake spiders all over the sheet.

They didn't want to piss me off too badly, or those bastards would have been real. Then I would have had to burn the bed down. Possibly the cabin too.

After cleaning it off, I get to work.

Almost an hour passes, and I already have three out of four of my jobs done for the week. I'm on a roll, when there's suddenly a pounding at my door. A very loud, very angry pounding.

"You assholes are not getting in! You promised on the graves you'd leave me alone!"

I grab my BB gun from beside the couch, pumping it once, preparing for battle.

"It's me. Put the gun down and open the door."

Benson.

I glance around, wondering if he can somehow see me through the solid door. My windows have curtains blocking out the sun, keeping the glare off my laptop.

Apparently he just knows me really well, since there's literally no other way he could know what I'm doing.

Warily, I put the laptop aside, then creep to the door and unlock it. Before I can get it all the way open, he's shouldering his way inside.

My breath leaves in a rush as he grabs my waist with one hand, and his other hand tangles in my hair, tugging my head back seconds before his mouth finds mine.

His tongue…*I think I love his tongue*, I decide, when it starts doing indescribably wonderful things to mine — teasing me, taunting me, fueling me.

I moan into his mouth as the kiss grows more aggressive, and my hands slip up to his shoulders as he presumably kicks the door shut.

He starts walking me backwards, still devouring my mouth, and I clutch him closer, drinking him in just as hungrily.

Maybe I read the situation wrong this morning, because this does not feel like a guy who regrets telling me he wanted me.

He lifts me, moving toward the bedroom, then pauses when he breaks the kiss.

I take the chance to breathe and look at his face. I'm so glad I can finally see his face, because those lips are perfect. I really love those lips.

"They fixed your bed," he says, causing me to blink and try to get some senses back.

"Yeah," I tell him, sounding breathy and girly at the same time.

He looks around warily. "Did you check under the sheets?"

"Fake spiders. They're gone."

He nods, still looking around.

"What about under the bed?"

"Nothing there."

"You're sure?"

I reach up and grab a handful of hair on the back of his head and drag his mouth back down to mine. He groans, and his hands go back to gripping me and walking me backwards.

My knees touch the bed, and he starts lowering me to it. We slide onto it together as he starts tearing at my shirt.

"Get naked," I demand, and he grins against my lips.

"Not until you tell me why you snuck out."

I gawk at him. "Are you kidding?" I ask incredulously, causing his eyebrows to go up.

At his oblivious stare, I realize he's not kidding.

"You came out of the bathroom, took one look at me, and suddenly you looked as guilty as I felt for eavesdropping. Then you disappeared downstairs without saying a word. I figured it was like all the times before — after you woke up from being drunk, where you regret getting handsy, only this time you also confessed something you didn't mean."

He studies my eyes, then his gaze rakes over my face. "You're painfully beautiful in the mornings," he says randomly. "Especially when you're on my bed, looking lost and expectant."

He blows out a breath, his lips brushing mine again. "I don't say the right things, or you'd have been in my bed even when I had a bad beard."

I laugh, caught off guard by that confession.

He smirks. "So I figured I'd get everyone out of the damn house and show you exactly how good this could be between us. I didn't want to risk saying the wrong thing."

I grin like an idiot. Oh, now I get why Delaney likes this dating thing so much. I've never been much of a goofy grinner until this moment.

"Well, not saying anything at all was the wrong thing too."

He snorts, then rolls his eyes. "So I've noticed."

He pushes up off the bed, and I lean up on my elbows to watch him as he tugs off his untied boots. My heartbeat gets faster as he pulls his shirt over his head, and my eyes hungrily rake over his body.

I can feel him watching me as I watch him shove his sweats down to his feet. No boxers. Yay!

Oh!

Wow…

"I hope you're on birth control," he says.

Remember how I thought Liam was freakishly gorgeous? Well, Benson is freakishly physically perfect. Like, even his penis is a work of art.

I almost don't understand his words, because I'm staring at that very hard, very large, perfect penis.

"I am," I murmur dumbly.

He stalks to me, and my breath leaves when he jerks my shorts down my legs, surprising me with his roughness. When I look up, I see the desperation in his eyes, and it matches mine.

As he drags my shorts off my legs, I throw my shirt over to a corner, baring myself completely to him. He comes down on top of me, his lips finding mine again as I buck against him, searching for that perfect penis.

"Fuck, I can't believe this is finally happening," he groans against my neck, spreading my legs wider.

Trying to form a response becomes impossible when his head suddenly dips and disappears between my thighs. One swipe of his tongue has me forgetting the English language.

Two swipes of his tongue has me forgetting my name.

Three swipes of his tongue has me only remembering his name.

When he fastens that incredible mouth around my clit, I become a writhing, wild animal beneath him. He growls against me, holding my hips down, and the vibrations only add to the stimulation that is driving me wild.

My hips try to buck, but he continues pinning me to the bed, forcing me to feel every incredible bit of what he's doing. It's been three years since someone other than myself worked me toward orgasm, so I'm not ashamed when I come like an unpracticed virgin within barely a few minutes.

My hands grip his hair, trying to push him back as my entire body shudders over and over.

He finally caves and starts kissing his way up my body, and my mind idly wonders why I couldn't have slept on top of him sooner. We could have been doing this all along.

His tongue circles my nipple, and then he shows it a little more attention when he sucks it into that talented, relentless, giving mouth. I mumble something like praise, gripping his hair and forcing him closer as my legs come up around his hips.

I'm strong, but not strong enough to force his body down to mine. His cock teasingly brushes my thigh as he keeps our bodies separated, moving his blessed mouth to the other nipple to show it some attention.

"Never hide that mouth again," I moan, causing a small chuckle to escape his lips.

His lips leave my nipple and find my lips again, and I kiss him hungrily, desperately, needing all of him.

His hand snakes between us, and my breath hitches as he lines us up in the best possible way and thrusts in. Considering how wet I am, it's not hard for him to sink almost fully in me with that one thrust.

He breaks the kiss to groan, his body going tight, then thrusts again, pushing the rest of him inside me as he shudders.

"I just realized how long it's been since I've been with anyone," he murmurs through strain. "Very possibly longer than three years."

I grin, actually loving that confession.

"Hence the reason you don't have a supply of condoms on hand," I say, though the words sound breathy and winded.

He kisses me again, withdrawing and thrusting back once more. His body feels so tight, and I know he's struggling. I break the kiss, smiling as I tug his head back.

"I've had an orgasm. Stop worrying. We can have sex more than once," I say with a smile, while he narrows his eyes in challenge.

"You can have another one with me."

His hand slips between us, and my smile dies, making room for my lips to form an "o" as his thumb finds my clit and starts making lazy circles as he thrusts in again.

My hands go everywhere, trying to touch him, mark him, feel as much of him as possible, as he continues to set a rhythm that borders on mind-blowing.

It passes that border when my next orgasm crashes through me like a tidal wave, hitting every nerve in my body as I cry out. He thrusts harder and harder, dragging out my orgasm in the best possible way as he puts both hands beside my head to leverage himself up.

I'm still rambling in some foreign language, when suddenly…an ominous *creak, pop,* and *snap* tries to warn us. But we're both too wrapped up in each other to even react as the bed plummets, crashing into the floor.

Benson doesn't even stop thrusting as the bed frame collapses around us, falling into the walls and thankfully not us. It actually turns me on more, especially when I watch his face.

It's sweet agony that would have been hidden from me if we'd done this in the past when his face was a mystery. I'd never want to miss that expression, because it makes me feel powerful, entranced, and possibly intoxicated.

This man has an incredible "o" face.

His body shivers against mine as he stays at the deepest point inside of me, and he drops to me when his arms give out. I wind my arms around his neck, kissing the side of his cheek that I can reach, as he pants for air.

"You're perfect," he says softly.

"You too."

I grin like a fool, and he kisses a spot on my neck near my ear.

I've had sex. I've had emotionless, hot sex. But never before have I felt anything like what I'm feeling now.

I was wrong to think I could live without something like this. Something *real*. Something worth more than a little fun.

And it's worth everything that will follow. Hopefully.

"Benson!"

We both go stiff, and Benson lifts his head to stare down at me, still inside me, as horrified humor lights his eyes.

"Benson Nolans!" Killian calls again.

Then Hale adds, "Get your cherry-popping ass out here right now! It's time to suffer."

Chapter **11**

Wild Ones Tip #23
If a Wild One is screaming, just walk away.
Trust me, we're not dying.

LILAH

I walk out after cleaning up, tying my robe as I glare at my soon-to-be dead brothers.

Killian is tapping a bat's end into his palm, and Hale is propped up on a shotgun.

"I'll give you one minute to get back to your cabin. One minute before I grab the BB gun. Then I'll have no mercy," I warn them.

Killian's eyes narrow.

"He took your virginity right next door! We heard you!" Hale shouts.

"I wasn't a virgin, you creep!" I groan.

"Yes. Yes, you were. And you will be again, as long as you don't have sex for a while," Hale says with so much conviction that I honestly believe he thinks it's the truth.

"My hymen will never grow back," I dryly remind them.

They both turn pale. "Sick! Stop talking about that," Killian groans.

"Me?! You're the two baboons who are in my front yard, assuring me that I'll be a born-again virgin after admitting to eavesdropping on me having sex!"

"You scared the entire forest! We weren't eavesdropping! Hell, we had pillows over our ears when you were making those nightmarish sounds that will forever haunt us!" Hale barks.

Okay, now that's kind of embarrassing.

Benson walks out, fully dressed, and they both tense as he pinches the bridge of his nose. "You guys are seriously going to pay for ruining this."

"You're going to pay for de-flowering our baby sister!" Hale shouts.

Killian nods as though he agrees with that ridiculous declaration.

"I'm two minutes older than you," I say to Hale. "And one minute older than you," I go on, gesturing to Killian. "I'm the oldest."

Hale sniffs, shoulders straightening. "It's a man thing, Lilah. Step aside."

My eyes narrow, but a hand clamps around my mouth before I can say anything. Benson's body presses up behind me, and I struggle to remove his damn hand.

"Even you two assholes can't possibly think your sister is always going to be single," he tells them. They exchange a look as he continues. "She's beautiful, smart, independent, and she's honest."

Okay, I admit I stop struggling to remove his hand for a minute so I can swoon. But it's brief. I go back to trying to pry that hand off again, realizing just how strong Benson is when it's a vain attempt.

"And you can't be oblivious to the fact I care about her. And I'm never leaving Tomahawk. Until now, she's never been intimate with anyone from Tomahawk. Would you rather her find someone not in this town? Someone who might take her away from it permanently?"

To this, they both pale, as if they hadn't considered the fact I might ever leave them. Which I wouldn't. They drive me crazy ninety-nine percent of the time, but they're still my brothers, and they love me in their own unusual way, just as I love them. I'd never abandon them.

However, Benson is making a point, and my brothers are less aggressive and more passive in the moment. Which is a first.

"That's what I thought," Benson says, his lips twitching as he removes his hand. "So are we going to have any more problems?"

Again, the duo exchange a look, doing that silent communication thing they do. Sometimes I'm in on it with them, but usually it's me silently shouting *no* at whatever destructive plan I can see brewing.

They look back at Benson, and their eyes creepily narrow in unison. "We'll have a big problem if you hurt her," Killian says.

Hale makes a point of slashing a finger across his neck. Benson's lips twitch.

"Understood."

They both toss me a glare before walking back to their cabin, but Hale turns around and points at us before he fully retreats.

"No more sex in your cabin. And we're not fixing that bed again. He broke it this time."

Then they turn around and leave us in peace.

"Well, that went better than expected," I say in surprise.

"I cheated by playing on their worst fear," he says, smirking as he rests his elbows on my porch railing.

He looks sexy on my porch.

Benson Nolans is actually the epitome of sexy, by my definition.

I lean up against him.

"I'd never leave them."

"I know that now. I didn't used to, but I do now. You're true to Tomahawk until you die."

He flashes a grin at me.

"You too?"

He nods, wrapping an arm around me.

"The worst is yet to come," I say on a sigh, and his eyebrows furrow. "Aunt Penny is going to find out about this. Then...the pressure begins."

He rolls his eyes. "It can't possibly be that bad."

Chapter 12

Wild Ones Tip #369
A Wild One is always right. Unless they're wrong.

LILAH

"Oh, the wedding should be here. At the house. It's where you two met, after all," Aunt Penny is saying, while I force a straight face.

Benson is surprisingly not ruffled by the thousand and one wedding details Aunt Penny has been rattling off for the past hour. We've literally been dating for two days, and she has our wedding planned.

Told you.

"I bet all of Tomahawk would come out to see these two tie the knot," my uncle chimes in before taking another drag off his pipe.

The pipe tobacco is permeating the air, even though we're outside. At our picnic table. I'm leaning against Benson as I've done for years, but it means something different than it used to.

And his arm is around me, because we can't stop touching. It's even worse than when we were just friends. I don't think we've stopped touching each other in some way unless bathroom breaks were required.

Benson's lips find my forehead, and I close my eyes, soaking it in. Until there's a terrifying squeal.

We both look at my aunt, who is clutching her hands together and staring at us with hearts in her eyes. That weird sound was apparently her vocalizing her excitement and not the sound of a cat losing its tail.

"You're so beautiful together. It's just lovely. It takes me back to when Bill and I first got together. I can't wait to see you in your mother's dress."

My heart thumps, and I tense, but Aunt Penny keeps on talking.

"I can alter it, if you want. But I don't think we should make any major changes. It would look so beautiful on you just as it is."

I offer her a tight smile in response. This pressure is only going to get more suffocating.

"I think we're just going to take it one day at a time for a while," Benson says, trying to keep the wedding planner at bay. "We've only just started dating," he reminds her, like a sane, rational person would.

She bats a hand. "You two love each other. You've been friends for years. You wouldn't be in a relationship now if it wasn't the real thing. I never thought it'd happen unless I kept trying to fix her up with guys."

To this, Benson and I look at each other, confused, before glancing back at her.

"Say what now?" I ask.

Her mischievous smile spreads, and my uncle laughs under his breath before he answers that question.

"She knew you weren't interested in anyone she brought out. She kept picking all those pretty boys for a reason. Benson wasn't making a move, but you two would practically be in each other's pockets when a potential suitor was involved.

Your aunt figured she'd push Benson along, hoping he'd finally break."

Benson frowns. "That's not what happened."

"In a way it was," Aunt Penny says, delighted with herself.

"Actually, it was my brothers wrecking my bed that did it."

Her face falls, and I feel like I've stolen something from her.

"That was what did it for her. For me, it was Liam coming into the picture," Benson lies. He's already told me the real moment he started having feelings for me that crossed the friendship line.

But it perks my aunt right up, and I want to kiss him for giving her that. My uncle winks at him like he knows what just happened too.

And I want Benson to myself for a while now so I can reward him properly.

"We need to go. I have some jobs to finish up," I tell her, tugging at Benson's hand.

He's quick to leap to his feet, ready to get out of here too.

"Oh, I'll make some wedding cake samples to see which is your favorite!" Aunt Penny calls out as we hurriedly make our way to the boat.

"Sounds good," I say over my shoulder, not slowing down.

As soon as we're pulling away from the dock, I look over at Benson. "Told you."

He laughs under his breath. "It wasn't as bad as you made it sound."

"I'll remind you of that when we come over for dinner one night, only to realize it's a surprise wedding and she's shoving us both down the aisle."

He laughs, but I'm not kidding. It's totally something she would do.

I watch him as he grins, relaxed in his seat like we didn't just endure an hour of wedding plans after *two days* of dating.

"You know my family so well, and I know nothing at all about yours," I say over the roar of the motor.

His smile disappears instantly.

We coast to his dock, and he starts tying off. I wonder if he's about to dismiss me the way he usually does when I pry.

"My family isn't like yours. Your brothers may drive you crazy, but they'd never hurt you or wrong you in any way. They have your back no matter what."

I finish tying off the back of the boat, and he lifts himself out before turning to offer me a hand.

"Are you saying you have a brother?"

He nods slowly. "Our relationship is likely beyond repair, but for a few weeks out of every year, we pretend we don't hate each other for the sake of our mother. Those are holidays that I go home, vacation weeks they come out here, and special occasions when I go to visit them."

My stomach flips, because it's the first time he's ever shared anything about his family. I knew he visited them, because I always go through withdrawals when he leaves Tomahawk.

Seriously, I don't know why I didn't consider my feelings for him sooner.

He looks around, rubbing a hand over the back of his neck. He grabs my hand, and he doesn't meet my eyes as he guides me onto the bank then up those fifteen steps to his door. But he talks while we walk.

"I moved out here because I needed a change, something that didn't remind me of everything that had happened. Hell, I wasn't here hardly five days before your uncle showed up, introduced himself, and told me there was a beard challenge. Then he informed me of the consequences if I didn't accept."

He grins like he's thinking back, and I grin too, because I can actually see it in my mind.

"Even though I kept to myself, I still started growing that damn beard. It was just too ludicrous of a request to ignore. And before I knew it, I belonged to Tomahawk. It fit me. And I never wanted it tainted with my past. I never wanted to give up what this place gave me back. And so…I never told anyone anything about my past. It was better to be a mystery than an open book."

He guides me inside his house, and I follow behind him, unsure how much to press for.

"What happened between you and your brother?" I decide to ask.

He turns to face me, blows out a breath, then gestures for me to sit down with him. I do, but he pulls me into his lap, nuzzling my neck with his nose.

"A woman."

I tense. Obviously.

I suddenly hate asking any questions.

"I dated a girl in high school," he goes on, "and the night of senior prom, right before we left in the limo, I got down on one knee and proposed to her."

Yeah…can't breathe. He proposed to someone?

I don't even know her and I hate her. Which is a new brand of crazy I'm not used to. It's also annoying, because I liked thinking of Benson as a virgin — no, I'm not delusional. It was just my fantasy.

"I thought we were in love. Hell, she was the only girl I'd ever been with." He keeps talking into my neck, and I'm thankful he can't see the inane panic on my face.

"She said yes. I should mention she was six months pregnant at this time," he says, leaning back to look into my eyes.

My heart plummets. He has a kid?!

Dizzy and lightheaded, I sway a little on his lap.

"Almost four months later, my kid was born. Or so I thought. My mother insisted on a paternity test, because she was convinced Sadie was lying. I went along with it just to prove her wrong. Sadie was reluctant, but she agreed. She regretted that when the paternity test showed the baby wasn't mine."

This time, my heart plummets for a different reason, because he looks away. I can practically feel his pain vibrating off him.

"I'd already baby-proofed our house — my mom's house. I still lived at home. She already lived with us, and my mother was going to help us raise our kid while we went to college. It definitely shattered me to learn she'd been pregnant with another man's baby — had cheated on me. I was still debating on if I could forgive her for the sake of the kid…but it was twice as devastating when she announced the baby was my brother's."

My arms wrap around his neck, and he tugs me closer, kissing my cheek. "Decision made that I couldn't get past either betrayal, I moved out here to escape all that. Instead, found somewhere I actually belong."

His eyes meet mine again, and I brush my hand along his jaw, feeling that soft hair there.

"I'm sorry. I had no clue."

He gives me a grim smile. "I didn't want anyone knowing. You're the first person I've told since moving out here. I'd appreciate it if it stayed between us."

I mime the motion of zipping my lips, and he smiles again, a real one this time.

"I'm an awesome secret keeper," I remind him.

His eyes narrow playfully. "I know. You never would tell me that it was your brothers who sank my canoe."

Because it wasn't my brothers. It was me. I didn't mean to shoot it. I was aiming at the damn woodpecker that was making my life hell, but tripped over my boot's untied shoelace as I fired the shot.

But, since I'm an awesome secret keeper, I keep that to myself and just grin at him.

"What happened between your brother and your ex?" I ask before I can stop myself.

That small bit of humor dies. "Nothing. My brother wasn't actually the father. That was just Sadie's way of tearing us apart by getting him to confess he'd screwed her behind my back. The baby belonged to another guy who eventually married her. But Sadie's marriage ended this past year."

I nod, even though I don't know why I'm nodding. I guess I'm not sure what else to say.

"One more thing," I say, prompting him to sigh.

"I think I've told you most of the drama that is my family. I don't really feel like saying more about it today."

I shake my head. "How do you make your money? I've Googled Benson Nolans a thousand times, and nothing ever pops up on you."

His grin instantly returns. "You've Googled me a thousand times?"

I nod, unashamed.

"I admit that I was mostly curious about what you looked like without a horrible beard — obviously this was before you lost it."

He chuckles under his breath.

"That's because I legally changed my name to Nolans before moving here. That was my grandmother's maiden name. My father hasn't been in the picture for a really long time, and that name would have pulled up some interesting things, if anyone from Tomahawk got curious and started asking questions."

"Why would you care?" I ask, confused.

He grins broader. "Because this is Tomahawk."

I groan as he laughs.

"Then what's your real name?"

He stands, putting me on my feet, before tugging my hand in his.

"My real name is Benson Nolans. It's the only name I care about. Everything before this version of me feels like a different person in a different life."

"You're not going to tell me, are you?" I ask as he starts guiding me upstairs.

He turns his head and flashes that devilishly perfect smile at me.

"The secret to being a bore is to tell someone everything."

When I groan again, he laughs, practically dragging me up the stairs to his bedroom.

I suddenly don't give a damn about his past when he presently starts kissing me stupid. I sigh into his mouth, too content to let this moment slip away, when his arms come around my waist and lift me so that he doesn't have to bend.

He lowers me to the bed before undressing me, and I push his clothes off him as fast as I can. I'm almost crazy with need when he finally pushes into me.

His lips stay on mine as his lazy thrusts do unpredictably awesome things to my body. I never knew how right something could feel.

In this moment, everything is perfect.

Chapter **13**

Wild Ones Tip #842
We're fucking crazy. Your crazy will never beat our crazy,
because we're competitive.

LILAH

"**Y**ou two are simply adorable," Evette Dickens says as I put some grapes into the shopping cart.

"Thanks," I tell her sweetly, letting Benson tug me to his side.

Evette's daughter is eyeing him, even though she's only sixteen. I admit, I totally get it. Benson is hot, and the world is starting to take notice that he's also awesome.

I still hiss at her like a rabid cat when she bites her bottom lip suggestively.

Evette's eyes widen, and her daughter pales, probably remembering I'm one of the four corners of crazy in Tomahawk for a reason.

Evette starts urging her daughter along as I chuckle to myself. Benson shakes his head, not even commenting on the fact I hissed. Then again, it's probably the least crazy thing he's witnessed me do.

We barely make it to the frozen goods, when we're abruptly cut off by Janice Holland, local busybody.

"I heard you two had finally crossed that threshold into couple-dom. How are your brothers handling it?" she asks

119

me, not bothering with small talk, since she's looking for something juicy to share about our corner.

"They're planning to make Benson an honorary Vincent," I say cheerily.

Benson grunts, not saying much as he starts grabbing food. He usually only talks regularly to me, and he doesn't say too much to people he doesn't know. Or like, for that matter.

"Really?" she asks, almost sulking like she's disappointed in the lack of crazy.

"I had to work three years to get into their good graces before I could be with her," Benson says, saving my brothers' reputations.

He doesn't turn around or even glance at her, and when her eyes rake over his profile, I cock my head.

"Anything else?" I ask, smiling the creepiest smile I have in my arsenal.

She clears her throat and looks back at me, recovering her fake smile.

"Are you two planning on tying the knot soon? I figured Penny would be sending out invitations already."

Benson chuckles, and her smile wavers. She expected that to scare him. Really, the guy has been dealing with my family for so long that it's a little hard to scare him.

"I think we'll fornicate for a while longer before spending money on some rings. I like it when he uses his tongue. Wouldn't want him getting lazy anytime soon just because of a piece of jewelry telling him I'm his."

Benson chokes on air, not turning around, as Janice's face turns three shades of red.

"I...think...Oh! I see Clara. I need to go there. To her. Now," she says rapidly, stumbling over all her words.

She's gone in the next instant, and I grab some frozen peas. A bunch of them.

"Why all the peas?" Benson asks, recovering from the way I dismissed our annoying busybody stalker.

"Great for sore balls," I state absently.

He groans as I toss in a couple more packs.

"Why?"

"I forget you don't shop with me usually. But the thing is, my brothers piss me off a lot. And when it's two-to-one, I have to capitalize on their greatest weakness. I also feel guilty every time I do. Therefore, I buy frozen peas."

He blows out a breath, like he's tired of trying to understand me, and I guide him through the store as he pushes the shopping cart.

"Speaking of which, why are you shopping with me today?" I ask him as we turn the corner to the chocolate aisle — A.K.A. the heavenly aisle.

His eyes come up just as Chuck comes walking down the aisle. At least I think it's Chuck. I'm still getting used to real faces and not figuring them out based on the beard.

Chuck's gaze drops to my legs, just as Benson's arms come around me, his hand possessively spreading over my hip.

"Chuck," he says, nodding politely despite the edge to his tone.

"Benson." He nods by way of greeting, since Benson's hands are too occupied with my body to offer a handshake.

"Heard you two were thinking of tying the knot," Chuck says, eyes lingering on my chest for a minute.

121

I'm wearing a T-shirt of a little woodpecker flipping a feathery bird finger. No cleavage to be seen.

"We're together," Benson says vaguely.

Chuck walks away, and I contemplate just how weird that all was.

"Well, that's why," Benson grumbles, tossing in my favorite chocolates.

He really is perfect.

"Why what?" I ask, confused.

"Since the beardless party, all the men have a double shot of ego and confidence. I've been jealous since before you were mine. I sure as fuck can't stand the thought of someone hitting on you now."

I grin before I can help myself, and he turns to face me, arching an eyebrow.

"You may *actually* get dubbed an honorary Vincent if you keep acting like one."

He cocks his head, studying me. "You saying you get jealous?"

"I hissed at a sixteen-year-old girl not ten minutes ago for giving you *the* eye. And I thought about rearranging Lindy's face with a beer bottle before cutting off her vagina lips. You forget I'm a corner of crazy."

His smile is instant, and I press against him as his arms come around me.

When his lips brush mine, I get lost for a minute, forgetting we're in the one and only grocery store.

"Let's hurry up and get out of here," he whispers across my lips, never kissing me, as though he knows—like I do—

that a kiss will lead to the inevitable indecent exposure that will get us banned.

Like my brothers.

Who I have to shop for.

We finish our shopping trip quickly after that, and stop at the hardware store, where I get left in his truck, because he knows there will be more men he'd have to show his jealous side to.

Since I find it cute, I let it slide, especially since he's buying the necessary items to fix my bed once and for all. It'll support two people's weight from now on.

We're almost back to my place when I decide I can't take it any longer, and start kissing my way up his neck, sliding across the single-cab bench seat to push right up against him.

He shifts gears, groaning as my hand starts undoing his jeans. My smile spreads when I feel him pulling off the road, and in the next instant, his hands are on me, tugging me onto his lap as he kisses my lips.

My ass hits the horn, but he flips the lever, pushing the steering wheel up enough to give me more room to work. Our kisses are frantic, almost like we're two teens in a hurry to get to the good stuff.

I can't seem to help myself as I get his pants worked down.

My skirt slides up with ease, bunching around my waist, and he groans when he realizes…no panties.

"Really? You've been walking around like this all day?" he says, his voice strained as I finally free him from his boxers and stroke his cock in my hand.

It's already hard, so there's not much prep work involved.

"You forget, I still have no underwear."

"Because of bugs," he murmurs, grinning as his lips find mine again, and his tongue takes control as I slide down on top of him.

We both break the kiss to take a deep breath as I sink onto him completely, taking him inside, and roll my hips.

His hands go to my hair, holding my head as he stares into my eyes for a long, intense moment. I move again, and he holds the eye contact as I rise up and push down harder, faster.

That's when his lips seize mine hungrily again, and I pick up the rhythm, riding him as hard as I can, chasing that incredible release. The windows fog, the truck rocks, and we're a tangle of tongues, lips and hands, both of us trying to get our fill of the other.

When my orgasm tears through me, he grabs me by the hips, taking over, fucking me from underneath as I shiver and ride the wave of euphoria, unable to do anything but *feel*.

It's not until his body is shuddering, and he's gripping me too tightly, that I realize he's found his.

He goes lax underneath me, and I smile against his neck, kissing it.

"I should have been shopping with you all these years if this is what happens at the end of the trip," he says through his heavy breaths.

Before I can answer, there's someone tapping on the window. During the commotion, my skirt fell down around us, hiding the good stuff. Thankfully.

Obviously I can't move, because my skirt is all that's covering his naked middle right now.

Benson rolls down the window to reveal our lone officer of the law. And...Benson is slowly softening *inside* me. This is not awkward at all.

"Benson. Lilah. Think you two could *not* pull over on the side of the road unless there's better coverage next time?" Vick asks, annoyed.

I smile and nod, and Benson answers, "Sorry, Vick. Found out why shopping trips are a good idea today."

Vick grunts and rolls his eyes, muttering something about the beardless epidemic as he goes back to his patrol car.

Benson laughs while leaning his head back, and I kiss his jaw as his hands smooth up and down my back.

"Well, now everyone will be wondering if we're skipping the wedding and going straight to baby-making," he says on a long breath through his chuckles.

"We'll tell them we're practicing, but I'm not having babies. Multiples are a hell no."

He starts to speak, when we hear Vick griping at us through his car's speaker.

"Get off the road. Now."

I shift off Benson, laughing as he does his pants back up, and he reaches over, taking my hand and kissing it before he shifts gears and starts driving.

Again, perfect.

Chapter 14

Wild Ones Tip #361
Wild Ones don't notice the way people stare. But they will make your life hell if you want to be rude.

BENSON

Lilah bends over the bank on the far end, her ass in the air as she curses. I drink my beer, watching her ass without having to be sneaky about it.

Joey rolls up to the edge farthest away from her just as Lilah gets her whopper of a fish pulled in, bouncing up and down in joy, since it's a beast. I'm not looking at the fish, though. Eyes are still mostly focused on her ass.

It takes me several seconds to realize Joey's boat is loaded down with five girls, all of them in bikinis and soaking in the sun while it's warm.

Joey is posturing like he's the king of the world, and I roll my eyes, smirking when Lilah grins over at me, showing me her beast of a fish.

"Yo, Benson. You want to ride with us for a while?" Joey asks, gesturing to the boat.

"We're good here," I say dismissively. "That's her fifth fish, and she hasn't been at it long. Don't want to mess up a good thing."

He rolls his eyes. "I wasn't inviting the Vincent. I have other company." He gestures to Tonya Murphy, who gives me a sly wave. "Tonya asked for you personally to join us."

"What'd he say?" Lilah calls from the other side of the bank as she starts walking toward us, dragging her string of fish with her.

Just as she nears, I grin and say, "Says he wants me to ride with him and his entourage, but you're not invited. Tonya's idea."

Joey darts a wide-eyed, panicked glance at me as he pales, horrified like I've betrayed him.

Lilah just smirks at him as she moves out onto the dock, getting closer to where they're idling.

The girls all pale as well, and Tonya starts hissing for Joey to get them the hell out of there.

As Lilah pulls off one of the still-live fish, she winks at him.

"Hey, Joey. Remember that time Tonya there puked all over the fire station?" Lilah asks.

"The great Vomit Massacre of 2010," I say, smirking.

Joey gives her a wary look, as Tonya squirms, eyeing the fish in Lilah's hand.

As if he figures out what's about to happen, Joey starts to gas his boat in reverse, and Lilah launches the fish. It smacks Tonya right in the face.

You can guess what happens next.

Tonya gags immediately, and turns right to Joey on instinct...and sprays all her lunch on him.

Joey curses, the boat veers hard to the right, tossing him off and killing the motor, as Tonya continues to cover the rest of the boat. Fortunately for the fish, one of the girls throws it off the boat, hoping to end the rancid upheaval, to no avail. And the fish swims away while the boat ride from hell stalls.

I turn away. My stomach isn't exactly iron-clad or anything.

Lilah already has her string of fish back in the water, and is now fishing off the dock, grinning as she watches the spectacle.

Life couldn't be better.

Chapter **15**

Wild Ones Tip #238
It's rare we have feelings. Don't fuck with them when we do.

LILAH

"How in the hell did you do this?" I snap, glaring at the two idiots who are looking anywhere but at me as Benson works on fixing my front porch.

He casts a glare in their direction, but they continue to whistle and stare at the sky.

"Answer me," I demand.

Hale finally blows out a breath.

"Fine. If you must know, we thought we'd conduct an experiment to see if buckshot was stronger than birdshot."

Killian smirks. Hale feigns contrition.

"You're serious," I say, staring between them. "And you conducted this experiment on my porch?"

Killian shrugs before grumbling, "You're never here anymore. Saw no harm in it."

So that's what this is about?

For the past two weeks, I've been at Benson's, basically living with him, since he never wants me out of his bed. We've only been coming out here to fix things when they're torn up—like my bed.

It's been great.

For me.

Apparently my brothers are a little jealous.

"What if we did a dinner tonight at my place?" I ask them, feeling a small pang of sympathy laced with guilt.

They both shrug. "That would be nice," Killian finally admits, still not making eye contact with me.

"And I'll make peach cobbler," I concede on a long breath.

This has both of them smiling.

"Go shower. You stink. And don't shoot at my porch—or house at all—ever again."

They both hug me, and I hold my breath, because they really do stink. Obviously they've been fileting fish all day or something. Then they jog off to their house to get showered.

"So I'm fixing your porch that they destroyed, and you're cooking them peach cobbler," Benson says on a frustrated breath. "That's rewarding bad behavior. They're totally playing you just to get cobbler, by the way."

I grin as I come up behind him, and he tugs me to the ground in front of him as his lips seek mine. We kiss lazily, as though we have all the time in the world, until I break the kiss to explain.

"They're a little jealous."

"That's gross," he deadpans.

I shove at his chest while rolling my eyes. "Of you and me spending so much time together. They're used to having me around to drive insane. I'm sure they're bored to death without me."

He shakes his head as I get up, and he hammers in the last board. He's been working on this for half the day, while I scoured the woods for my brothers. When I found them, they didn't come back willingly.

I had to threaten to tell Uncle Bill what they'd done before they'd even drag their feet back.

They'd already bought the supplies to fix the porch, and left a note for Benson to finish the job.

Passive aggressive isn't their usual style.

"Well, I can't stay for dinner tonight, so they'll have you all to themselves," Benson says distractedly, packing his tools up.

My lips purse. Maybe I've grown clingy, because we haven't spent a second apart in two weeks, and now I don't want him to be away from me all night.

"What's going on tonight?"

He steps back to look at his handiwork before answering almost absently. "My family gets in tonight. They'll be here for a week, so I'll have to slip over and visit you when I can until they're gone."

He says it so matter-of-factly, as though this isn't a major shot to the gut. Like he didn't just make me feel like a dirty secret.

"Oh," I say, trying not to sound as deflated as I feel.

I still don't know how wealthy his family is, but I estimate it's very wealthy, based on the tidbits of information he's shared over the past two weeks. It didn't bother me or even concern me, until now.

I never stopped to realize that a girl from Tomahawk, who wears combat boots with shorts, and braids her hair when she's too lazy to brush it, and usually goes without makeup, would be an embarrassing woman to introduce to someone's prestigious family.

I get it. I do.

Sort of.

It still stings though.

"Right," I say when silence fills the air.

"Anyway, I need to get back and get cleaned up before the yearly week from hell begins," he says, turning to face me with a tight smile.

I try to act like everything is cool, not like I'm embarrassed or suddenly feeling like I'm worth a little less to him.

He kisses me chastely, and I stare after him as he walks away.

At least now I realize why we drove both boats over here, instead of just taking one. He didn't want to leave me without my boat for the week.

How thoughtful.

Do I want to stab something? Maybe a little.

Do I want to shoot my new porch he just fixed to be petulant? Maybe a lot.

Instead, I turn and walk into the house, refusing to dwell on it, grab the spare keys to Killian's Jeep, and walk over to borrow it.

I also understand why Benson fixed my bed now, even though I didn't have any plans of sleeping on it for the foreseeable future.

It's not like I expected to spend every waking moment together. Okay, so maybe I did. Which is ridiculous, really. I, who never wanted a serious relationship, is upset about not being good enough to meet the family.

"I bet his family sure as hell wouldn't be pressuring me for marriage," I mutter to myself. "They'd probably sanitize their hands after touching me."

Miffed, degraded, and feeling inadequate, I drive to the store to buy stuff to cook for my brothers.

At least they're not ashamed of me.

I'm shopping for all of five minutes when I run into Janice Holland, the town's busiest busybody. Benson was with me the last time I had to face her down.

"Oh! You look so pitiful, Lilah! Where's Benson?"

I force a smile. "He's at his house. He has his family over today, and I'm picking up some supplies to cook dinner for my brothers."

Her eyes ooze with mock sympathy, and I frown, wondering why in the hell she's feigning a sympathetic look at all. "Oh, it's okay, sweet girl. There are plenty more fish in the sea, and we all know you're a tigress on the prowl when you want to be."

I open my mouth to speak, when she continues.

"It's just that it's clear Benson's family is made out of a lot of money. I'm sure you understand why this had to be," she prattles on, twisting that invisible knife in my gut a little deeper.

I'm about to cunt punch her.

"Janice, you don't—"

"And don't you dare worry about people talking about it. Trust me. It'll pass," she adds patronizingly.

She pats my shoulder, and I say, "But we're not—"

"Shhh," she coos, putting her finger to my lips.

Does she want this *tigress* to bite that damn thing off? Because that's seconds away from happening. You don't touch a Vincent. This should be a widely known, well-documented fact.

"Don't worry, dear. Don't worry. This, too, shall pass," she essentially purrs.

She scurries off, practically riding that shopping cart toward the front, and I roll my eyes.

Stupid town.

Stupid people.

Stupid Benson.

Chapter 16

Wild Ones Tip #487
Wild Ones don't always think things through, and we like to act
before you can speak.
To hell with the words and stuff.

LILAH

"Die! Die, motherfucker!" Killian laughs at the TV as he
shoots Hale's avatar over and over.

"That's cheating!" Hale accuses.

I'm vaguely aware of them both as I peer through the
window with my trusty binoculars, trying to get a glimpse of
Benson's elusive family who are arriving now.

They're having to park around the side, since his
driveway is too small for too many cars. For once, I knew the
exact day—and time frame—they were coming, which has
upped my stalker game.

Does he have a sister too? Because I get a brief glimpse of
a woman who is too young to be his mother.

Why haven't I heard about a sister?!

Or maybe it's his brother's new girlfriend or something.

I hate that he doesn't want me there with him. I could
help keep him distracted from the brother drama he's stuck in.
I'd be an awesome distraction, as a matter of fact.

They disappear before I can be truly sure of anything, and I go back to the table to stab my fork at the cobbler. Or what's left of it, anyway. I forgot how much my brothers can eat.

"Is Benson coming over later?" Killian asks, his attention mostly focused on the TV.

"Just us tonight," I grumble.

"I need a new challenge. Hale is too easy to kill."

"Fuck you," Hale growls, just as the screen fills with blood and Killian cheers for himself.

Killian stands, and his phone rings on his hip. He flips it open—*yes, he has a flip phone*—and answers it.

"Hello?"

I start cleaning up the plates from dinner, and half-heartedly listen in.

"No. I don't think so…well, actually, that would make sense."

I glance over to see Killian's lips tense as his eyes darken. What's wrong?

"Thanks for telling me, Aunt Penny. Hale and I can handle this from here."

He hangs up and stalks toward me. Hale is right on his heels like he knows he's needed. Who's going to die?

"Did Benson break up with you?" Killian demands, and Hale's eyes narrow to slits.

"Is that why you've been so quiet and looking through the binoculars over there?" Hale adds immediately, his tone lethal.

"No…we didn't break up," I say carefully, knowing I'm navigating a landmine field right now.

"Then why do you look so crestfallen?" Hale asks seriously.

"Crestfallen? Did you actually just use the word *crestfallen* appropriately?" I ask, trying to distract him with something shiny.

"Answer the question," Killian growls.

I roll my eyes.

"His family is in town," I say with a shrug, trying to act like I'm not the least bit bothered by it.

"So?" they both ask at the same time.

"So, you know how he is. He doesn't let anyone meet his family."

Again I offer a one-shoulder shrug, and go back to washing the dishes like I enjoy it, as though I'm completely unaffected by the fact I'm too embarrassing to have around a fancy family.

"In other words, he has his family over, and they're too good for him to introduce you to them?" Killian snarls.

Okay, so my brother is a little more perceptive than I give him credit for being.

"That's not what this is," I grumble, not even sounding convincing to my own ears.

"Right. Excuse us," Hale says, and they spin on a heel and leave.

That's never a good thing.

Ever.

I quickly dry off my hands and tug on my boots, then grab my BB gun just in case, making it outside in time to see them walking toward the dock.

Killian has a bat over his shoulder. Hale has a shovel over his.

I pale.

"What the hell are you doing?" I bark, running after them as they get on the boat.

"Breaking something. Don't worry. We don't intend to kill him," Killian answers flippantly.

"Then what's the shovel for?" I yell as I run faster, trying to catch up before they take off.

"In case things get out of hand," Hale says with a smirk. "Shit happens."

I lunge just in time, landing in the boat as Killian gasses it away from the dock, and I start struggling with Hale, trying to take the shovel away.

"You're not doing this! Stop the damn boat!" I shout.

"No one acts like they're too good for our baby sister!" Hale barks.

"I'm your older sister! Stop the damn boat!" I shout at Killian.

He doesn't stop. He doesn't stop at all.

They're leaving me with no choice; I'm going to have to shoot them.

Chapter **17**

Wild Ones Tip #142
If you date a Wild One, you can't complain.
You knew you were getting mixed up in some crazy shit.

BENSON

My mother is the first to walk through the door, and her eyes widen in shock when she sees me.

"Benson! You finally got rid of that horrid beard."

I'm not lying when I say there are tears in her eyes. She practically squeezes my face in half when she gets her hands on me.

I'm vaguely aware of John, her husband, walking in behind her. Right behind him is my brother, who nods in my direction before disappearing out of sight. It always takes us a minute to be in the same room without me trying to kill him.

Usually.

But today, for some reason, I don't even care to see him.

Actually, I know what that reason is, and she's across the lake. I'm ready to find time to sneak out of here so I can go be with her.

Mom releases me just as Sadie walks in, and I take a steadying breath. Usually my chest hurts as residual betrayal slinks in and squeezes me, immediately followed by the need to wring her neck.

Not today.

Today, for the first time ever, I feel absolutely nothing when I see her.

No anger.

No hurt.

Nothing at all.

A small smile forms on my lips, and she takes it wrong, smiling back widely at me.

Shit. No bad beard. She's looking at me like she used to, and I'm smiling about the fact I'm in deeper than I even realized for Lilah. I'm *not* smiling at my ex. But she is smiling at me.

I break eye contact, clearing my throat as I look back down at my mother.

"How was the trip?" I ask her.

"Long. As always."

My nephew comes zipping in, his face glued to his phone. Absently I start wishing Lilah had a phone so I could text her right now…tell her I miss her already.

Because I'm so fucking far gone for her that I can't think straight without her.

For a solid year, I went over the pros and cons of going after her. The cons mostly being her family—in the event things didn't work out. They'd definitely make my life hell.

But the biggest con was losing her completely, when she'd somehow become the best part of my day. Now I wish I had just gone for it sooner, because the pros far outweigh the cons, and I could never go back to just being her friend.

I check to see if she's online as my mother and stepfather start walking their things in and telling Ryder—my nephew—

to get his things too. She's not online anywhere, unfortunately.

My brother reemerges just as the doorbell rings, and he opens the door on the road's side.

"Hello?" he says, sounding confused.

"Hey, I'm here to see Benson," a familiar voice says.

Shit. Shit. Shit.

I round the corner to see Lindy beaming at me with a covered dish in her hand, while Deacon — my brother — stares at me with an arched eyebrow.

Lindy looks like a stripper on her way to work. She normally doesn't dress like this. What's going on? She hasn't bothered me since the night of the beardless celebration.

After she thought Lilah was staking her claim, she backed off. As all the women did. Because…it's Lilah. She's a Vincent. You don't mess with a Vincent and expect to walk away unscathed.

"Hey," she says, smiling happily at me. "I heard about you and Lilah, and thought I'd bring you something to cheer you up."

My eyebrows have to hit my hairline.

"Heard about me and Lilah? What about us?"

"Who's Lilah?" my mother asks from somewhere behind me.

Lindy's eyes widen when my mother approaches, and I pinch the bridge of my nose. Now Lindy looks uncomfortable, since she didn't expect to be wearing a see-through top over a red bra, and daisy dukes in front of my mom.

Obviously.

She's usually fairly conservative…in groups.

"I...uh...I'll just give you a call later. What's your number?" she asks, as I start closing the door, not accepting the covered dish.

"Nothing happened between me and Lilah," I tell her as I shut the door on her protests.

When I turn around, everyone is looking at me.

"That's the first time anyone has ever come to your house when we've been here," Deacon decides to point out.

I pull out my phone, seeing Lilah still isn't online anywhere.

"I need to make a call," I grumble, moving away from them and not answering any questions.

"Who's Lilah?" my mother asks again.

"Yeah, Benson, who's Lilah?" Sadie drawls, but I ignore them all.

"Anyone want some wine?" I hear my brother asking.

Penny picks up on the first ring. "Hello," she says calmly, almost sounding a little eerie.

"Lindy just showed up at my house, presumably thinking Lilah and I broke up, and Lilah isn't online. Anyway, can you take your phone to her?"

"I'm afraid not. Her brothers are over there right now, and I'd fear for your safety if they learned you broke her heart. She hasn't even told me yet, but I heard from Jillian who heard from Karen who heard from Janice that she's been crying nonstop. I'm just waiting on those two knuckleheads to leave before I go over there."

What the fucking hell?

"I didn't break up with Lilah," I tell her. "And I can't picture Lilah crying. She'd be beating my head in with a frying pan, but not crying."

She makes a disgruntled sound. "She never wanted to date," she says on a sigh. "This is all my fault. I kept pushing her into it. Now you've gone and ruined her. I doubt she'll ever date again."

A long, sad sigh follows that, with a dramatic huff tacked on for good measure, letting me know she's truly disappointed in me.

"Penny, I swear to you, I haven't broken up with Lilah. And I don't want to," I growl, making sure no one can hear me as I go outside, eyeing Lilah's red flag that is waving in the air with a dead chipmunk on it.

An *image* of a dead chipmunk, that is. Not an actual dead chipmunk.

Why a chipmunk? Because the Wilders have raccoons on their yellow flags, and the Vincents are a tier or two below on the crazy corner scale from them.

Because this is Tomahawk.

It's how we do things.

Penny is silent for a moment. A really long moment.

"Just let me talk to her, please. I'm sure this is all one seriously screwed up misunderstanding."

She sighs long and loud. Again. "Is your family there? Is that why you can't go over there yourself? Her flag is up."

Sometimes I'd like to choke this woman…

"I know her flag is up. I can see it from here, which is why I asked you to go over there. And yes, I'm busy and can't go over there."

"Why wouldn't you invite her over if your family is there? Is my niece not good enough for them?" There's a harsh edge to her tone that I've never heard her use before.

"No. Of course not. It's nothing like that," I answer, confused about why she would even assume that.

"Then what is it?"

Shit. Shit. Shit.

"It's a long story. I need to talk to Lilah so I can stop worrying about—"

The door opens, and I look back to see my brother poking his head out. "There's a Janet here to see you. Says she brought cupcakes to help with your breakup."

"Janet Lowery?!" Penny screams in my ear, forcing me to hold the phone away or go deaf. "Janet is good enough for your family, but not my Lilah?! And everyone knows you don't bring cupcakes to anything but a celebration. That little brat is celebrating!"

Kill me now.

"No, Penny, that's not—"

"Fear the wrath of the Vincents, Benson Nolans," Penny seethes. "I'm turning them loose on you now. No more mercy."

She hangs up on me, and I quietly remind myself that I love Tomahawk because of the crazy people who live here. Though in this moment, I wish there was *some* sanity.

I stalk toward the front door where Janet is waiting. "I'll give you two seconds to leave, and I won't tell Lilah you showed up. We're still together."

Her eyes widen in horror before she drops the cupcakes and darts back to her Mustang, squealing out in reverse before her door even fully shuts. Another car is trying to pull up—I think it's Jessica Sparks—and Janet pokes her head out to yell at her.

"They're not broken up! Lilah will kill you! Or worse, turn her brothers loose!"

Typically, these girls would be considered the town's "mean girls," but in Tomahawk, crazy trumps mean any day of the week.

Jessica squeals out just as fast, the two vehicles narrowly dodging a collision with each other.

"For heaven's sakes, just who is this Lilah?" my mother asks, too intrigued for her own good now.

Annoyed, I go back to trying to figure out what to do. I need to just drive over there, but now isn't the best time. My family is already too curious about Lilah. The last thing I need is for them all to collide.

I should have just been upfront with Lilah about the complications, but it's a little fucking late for that now.

My doorbell rings as I try calling Bill, hoping he will be more practical than Penny.

"Run," is what he says when he answers. Then he hangs up on me before I can get a word in.

Oh, for fuck's sake.

"He's still with Lilah," I hear my brother saying, seconds before someone squeals and runs away. "That's just fascinating," he adds, amused as he shuts the door.

"What the hell is going on around here?" my stepfather asks, a small smile on his lips. "You finally back in the saddle, champ? Is that why you cut off that horrid beard?"

Sadie bristles, my brother smiles, and my mother claps her hands together in glee.

"I've been in the saddle for years," I point out dryly. "It's not like that. I'm dating someone—"

"Then introduce us to her!" my mother says excitedly. "Is she a local? I truly find them riveting."

She's going to regret that if Lilah's brothers really do show up. Mom doesn't understand the four corners of crazy in this town.

Surely Penny wouldn't do that to me. It had to be a bluff.

The doorbell rings again, and I try calling Killian—I'm desperate, obviously—but it goes to voicemail.

"He's still with Lilah," I hear my stepfather chirp, then he laughs when someone else squeals. "This is oddly fun. I can't wait to meet Lilah."

My mother gasps, staring out the window to the lake. "What?" I ask, still distracted as I try to dial Hale…and get voicemail.

"Two boys are being beaten to death by a girl near your steps on the bank," she answers in fascinated horror.

"Awesome," my nephew says, his face pressed to the glass as he gawks.

I rush to the wide, massive window, seeing the scene before me play out. Lilah is in cutoff jean shorts and a "Doc Holiday" T-shirt, as she shoots Hale with a BB, simultaneously kicking Killian in the stomach while he's on the ground.

Hale screams when she nails in him the nuts with another BB, pumping the Daisy for the next shot she aims at Killian when he tries to get up.

Her combat boots come up to her calves, pink laces made out of survival cords, and she kicks Hale in the kneecap this time, utilizing said boots like this is a war zone.

I idly notice the bat and shovel abandoned by the shore, and groan when I realize Penny did sell me out.

"Who on earth is she?" my mother asks as she looks on in guilty pleasure.

With a deep exhale, I answer, "*That* is Lilah."

Chapter 18

Wild Ones Tip #584
To piss off a Wild One, you have to really fuck up.
Then learn how to hide.

LILAH

"Stay down," I bark at my annoying brothers as they whine and pant from the ground.

Yeah, I have an unfair advantage, because they won't hit me back. And usually I don't exploit it, but today, lives are at stake. Mainly, Benson's. He owes me so big.

Now if I can just get us out of here before—

"Any reason why the entire town thinks we broke up?"

I close my eyes at the sound of the voice too close to my back. Damn it.

Until this moment, I saw no *real* reason for him to be ashamed of me. But now, I totally get it. I'd hide me too if my family was...not like my family.

I turn around as my brothers continue to groan on the ground, and drop the Daisy by my side as I look up at a very amused Benson.

"Sorry. Just help me get them into the boat, and we'll be out of your hair. I get it now. Really. I do. It might have taken this—" I gesture to the family I had to wrangle into submission. "—to make me see it, but now I see it."

His amusement dies, and his brow furrows. "See what?"

"Why you were too embarrassed to introduce me to your ritzy family."

A little humiliated, I turn around, kicking Hale when he glares at Benson. He grunts, crawling toward the shore.

"We'll get him later," Killian mutters petulantly.

They bump fists while continuing to crawl, but before we can make it to the dock, a hand clamps down on my arm, and my breath gets sucked out of me as Benson spins me back to face him.

He looks angry. I don't know if he's ever looked angry with me. At least not this angry.

"You think I'm too embarrassed to introduce you to my family?" he asks incredulously, and I shift uncomfortably.

"Well, yeah. Isn't that why you essentially told me to stay on my side of the lake while they're here?"

"Dead. He's dead," Killian groans, still trying to stand up.

Benson shakes his head, grunting something under his breath that sounds like *unbelievable.*

"No, Lilah. I'm not at all embarrassed about being with you. And I guess I should have elaborated, or at least tried to, but my family is a little more complicated than I explained. I just wanted to get this week over with, keep you out of the drama, and then it'd be just us again. In our motherfucking perfect bubble. I'm not embarrassed about you. I'm embarrassed about them."

A small smile tugs at my lips, and something suspiciously like tears fills my eyes. Maybe this was bothering me more than I care to admit. His look softens as he strokes my cheeks with such sweet affection.

"I can handle crazy," I assure him.

"Not crazy," he says on a sigh. "Complicated. There's a difference."

"So we don't have to kill him?" Killian asks disappointedly.

"You don't have to *try* to kill me," Benson tells him dryly.

"So we got our asses kicked for nothing?" Hale asks through strain.

"Looks like it," Killian grumbles.

I'm smiling up at Benson, slowly melting against his body as he tucks a wayward strand of dark hair behind my ear, when I notice movement. My eyes dart up to the porch on the hill, where four people are looking down at us.

Okay, now I'm really embarrassed. And that's hella hard to do.

An older woman and man are grinning down at us, while another man is studying us with an unreadable expression. Then the last one, the girl I don't know about, is stone-faced as she stares down.

"We have an audience," I whisper, feeling the red rise to my cheeks.

Benson freezes for a second before peering over his shoulder, seeing his family looking down on mine—*oh, the irony*—from the top of the hill where his house is.

"Hello, Lilah! We've just heard so much about you!" the older woman calls, waving at me with a *lot* of enthusiasm.

I suck in a breath and force a smile while waving back.

"Hello, Lilah's brothers!" she calls down.

"Hello, ma'am," they both manage to say in unison, still exhausted as they lie flat on their backs and pant for air.

"This is my husband, John," she says, gesturing to the older man beside her who gives me a thumb's up and a grin.

Okay…they're really accepting, obviously. They don't seem the least bit deterred by our little fiasco. I expected snooty people. And they also seem nice? What was Benson's problem with us meeting?

"And this is our son, Deacon," she says. I scowl before I can stop myself, and his lips twitch.

Benson's grip gets a little tighter on me too.

I notice a fifth face I hadn't seen, and my stomach gets a little tighter.

"Our grandson, Ryder," she goes on.

Grandson? I thought it wasn't Benson's kid. Or his brother's…

Did his brother have a child with someone else?

His mother hesitates her introductions on the girl who is still regarding me with no expression at all.

"And this is John's daughter, Sadie."

Sadie.

It's highly unlikely there are two Sadies in his life. He just forgot to mention that his ex is also his stepsister. And that she's going to be here for a week. And that's why it is complicated.

That's why I couldn't be here.

That's why he didn't tell me the whole story.

Just like that, the air is stolen from my lungs, and I cut my eyes toward Benson. It hurts to know he was going to spend the week with her, while shoving me to my side of the lake.

The only complications here were for him.

Unbelievable.

Benson's hand tightens on me, but I shrug him off. Sadie makes an expression for the first time, and it's a smile.

She knows.

I know.

And Benson knows.

We all know I'm an idiot.

Life is grand.

"As soon as you can move again, you can kill him," I tell my brothers, walking toward the dock.

"Lilah!" Benson growls, following behind me.

"Don't," I say, blowing out a breath as I look at him. My eyes flick over his shoulder as he continues to stalk toward me. "Don't embarrass me even more than I've already been embarrassed," I add.

He stops, freezing to his spot, as the first tear falls from my eyes. Both of my brothers purposely shoulder by him on their way to me, and I shake my head.

"Lilah, I swear to you, this is not—"

"I'm sure it's not," I say quietly, desperately ready to get the hell out of here. "But I guess I would have known that if you'd bothered to tell me. I need to go."

Hale reaches up, helping me into the boat, and Killian starts the motor. Just as he's about to pull away, I turn around, aim my gun, and shoot Benson right in the nuts.

He drops to his knees, cupping his balls as his face turns red, and I smile as I wave, reminding him who I am.

Yeah.

That's right.

I'm a Vincent.

We're one corner of the Wild Ones.

He really should have seen that coming.

Bastard.

Chapter **19**

Wild Ones Tip #567
Wild Women are worse than Wild Men. Because we'll kill any
fucker that puts their hands on a woman, which means they
constantly have the upper hand. You have to be creative to
one-up those vicious, untouchable little women.

BENSON

"I take it you didn't tell her Sadie was your stepsister," Mom
says on a sigh as I ice my balls down with frozen peas.

I grimace, shifting the peas. You don't think about a tiny
little BB hurting that badly. No wonder those pricks are so
tough. They've been conditioned by Lilah all these years.

"No, I didn't tell her that when I was sixteen I married
my girlfriend's father. I thought that would put a kink in our
new relationship to learn the woman I proposed to and
thought I'd knocked up was a permanent fixture in my life.
I'm Lilah's first real relationship because she's hard as hell to
get close to. Something like that just seemed like I was
pushing too much too fast."

She sighs as she stares out the window. "I blame myself
for this mess. I didn't mean to fall in love with John. Now you
and your brother hate each other. The girl who broke your
heart is still haunting your life, and it's all my fault."

"It's not your fault you fell in love. And John has a blind
spot for his daughter, just as you have a blind spot for us. As
for Sadie haunting my life, that's normally not an issue
anymore. I should have told Lilah everything and hoped for

the best. I just wanted more time to make sure she cared about me enough to overlook it. I should have known better than to think this wouldn't backfire, and I should have stopped to think what *she'd think* if I didn't explain why I didn't want her over here."

She turns to face me, her eyes sad.

"What are you going to do to get her back?" Mom asks with sincere concern.

I laugh humorlessly. "Everything I can. Don't worry. I have a fail-safe plan if all else fails."

Deacon walks in, no expression on his face.

"There's someone at the door for you," he says to me.

"Tell her Lilah and I are still together."

His lips tug into a half smile. "It's a guy. Says his name is Paul."

My brow furrows, but before I can ask questions, Paul is walking in, eyeing my brother and mother. No one from Tomahawk has ever seen me with them, and I usually force my family to stay out of sight.

It's Tomahawk. I'd never hear the end of it if everyone knew exactly how privileged my upbringing was. Or what my family is known for…

"Delaney called Killian after the rumor mill exploded. Lilah got on the phone and said you two broke up because she just couldn't do the settling down thing like she thought. I just came by to fix things, because if Delaney comes after you, I'll have to maim your face or something." He says all this as though it's just a normal conversation and no big deal.

My mother blinks in surprise, and my brother's smile grows.

"I'd hate to do that, since we're friends and all," Paul goes on conversationally. "But I really like Delaney, and I already feel like the runner-up since she originally went after you until she learned Lilah already had dibs."

"In all these years, I never realized just how interesting this town was," my brother says quietly.

Cursing, I shift the peas off my balls so I can stand up. "I've been in love with Lilah Vincent for almost a year. No, I don't want to steal Delaney from you. And yes, I do want to fix things with Lilah. Tell Delaney not to tell all the other beardless followers that Lilah dumped me. Got it?"

He nods, a smile curving his lips now.

"Got it." Then Paul's smile disappears. "How are you going to get past the brothers? You know they'll be ready to kick your ass if you start hassling her. You can fight, but there's two of them. And...they're Vincents. They won't hold back if Lilah lets them off the leash. And they won't fight fair if they're not on that leash."

I'm painfully aware they've never fought me dirty, which is why I always won. As long as Killian couldn't hit me with his mean right, I could kick their asses. One at a time.

Two at once in an unfair setting? My odds greatly depreciate.

"Actually...I need your help with that."

He pales. As expected.

"Nope. No. Not happening. I never want a Vincent coming after me. You're on your own."

"I can help," Deacon says, looking over at me.

My jaw grinds.

"I owe you this. I think it's time to…try to fix things. I'm also not scared of two guys who got their asses kicked by a girl," my brother goes on.

"A Vincent girl," Paul is quick to interject. He wasn't here, but he knows the drill without having seen it today. "They allow her to kick their asses."

I nod in agreement with him.

Deacon shrugs. "I'm sure I can handle it."

Considering I've always wanted payback, I have no qualms about sending him in unprepared.

"If you make her hate me worse, I'll kill you myself," I say with a pointed stare.

"I don't want her to hate you. I just want to help you fix this," he tells me earnestly.

Sadie walks by, and we all get quiet.

"What?" she asks, studying us. "Are you two talking about me?" she asks, her eyes narrowing as she points between me and Deacon.

"No. We're talking about Lilah," Paul says, frowning. "Who the hell are you?"

Her face relaxes. "Sadie."

He continues to stare at her. "Okay…but who are you?"

In that moment, Sadie's face falls, and she realizes she wasn't important enough for me to ever whine about when I ran off to this place. She blows out a breath before turning and walking away.

Deacon is practically beaming.

"So what do I do?" my brother asks, unaware of what's about to happen to him.

"Deliver a message."

"Can't you just call her?" my mother asks, confused. Hell, I forgot she's been listening to all this.

"Lilah doesn't have a phone," Paul supplies.

"Her flag is up, so I know she's at home right now," I go on.

"Her flag is up?" Deacon asks, eyebrows rising.

"Are you going to help or not?" I ask him, exasperated. I don't have the time or patience to explain Tomahawk to him right now.

"Two against two sounds like better odds, so I'm definitely going to help. What's the message?"

"Not today," Paul says, shaking his head. "The brothers won't leave her today. Wait until tomorrow."

As much as I hate the thought of giving her more time to stew, I know he's right. If I tried to cross the lake, they'd possibly throw pipe bombs at me.

I wish I was kidding.

"You think you could get them out tomorrow?" I ask him.

"Me? No. Delaney can though, as long as I explain that there's a really good reason for all this. There is a reason for all this, right? It's not just because Lilah is afraid to settle down?" Paul asks with a frown.

Yeah, no. I'm not telling him.

"Helping or not, Paul? In or out?"

"Delaney might come for him if you don't hurry up and help," my brother goads, not knowing anything at all about Delaney.

She'd never do that to Lilah. Even if she wasn't her friend, Delaney isn't suicidal.

A determined glint shades Paul's eyes. "I'm in."

I point a finger at Deacon. "Whatever happens…no matter what is said…do *not* tell Lilah my true last name."

"Why?" he asks slowly.

Sighing heavily, I answer, "Because this is Tomahawk."

Chapter 20

Wild Ones Tip #26
If your ass catches on fire, jump in the lake.
That's what it's there for.

LILAH

I'm not sure who I'm expecting when I swing open the door to find out who the hell is banging it so loudly, but it's certainly not Deacon—Benson's brother.

I pump my Daisy, aiming it at his forehead, and he holds his hands up as a smile etches across his face. A face too similar—but smoother with no beard at all—to Benson's.

Why is he smiling? Does he not realize this thing is loaded? I know it looks small, but it's pump action—Vincent style. It hurts like a bitch the more times I pump.

"Easy. I'm just here to talk," he says, still grinning.

"The last girl who dated Benson that you talked to announced she was pregnant with your baby," I remind him, feeling defensive of the bastard even as I hate him a little.

That turns his smile into a grimace. "Which is why I'm here on behalf of my brother now, to do the right thing for once."

"Tell me why you screwed his fiancée, and I'll consider not shooting you."

"Are all the women here like you?" he muses.

"Some are crazier," I say with a shrug, now feeling defensive of myself as I stand a little taller, pushing my shoulders back as though that somehow helps me look saner.

His grin spreads again, but it falls when he exhales harshly. "Fine. To be fair, they weren't engaged the first time I was with her. I wanted Sadie before my brother. We were sixteen—"

"Who's we?" I interrupt.

"All of us. Sadie, me, and Benson."

I lower the gun a little, keeping it pointed at his groin now. Which he subtly tries to cover. Guess he witnessed Benson's pain. That makes me feel a little better.

Wait? All of them were the same age? That means—

"You and Benson are twins?" I ask, that part of the puzzle suddenly snapping together.

"Fraternal twins," he says, frowning. "He didn't tell you that?"

"In case you haven't noticed, I wasn't told a huge chunk of family history."

He nods in understanding. "Right. Well, Sadie and I had been talking, but she ended up choosing my brother. I never told him I was into her, and I expected my feelings to go away. I mean, I was sixteen, so how tough could that be? But they didn't go away, since it became a game of wanting what I couldn't have—forbidden fruit and all that. Then one night they had a nasty fight, broke up, and she came to me."

He groans like he hates thinking back to it.

"I was almost seventeen at the time. She came to me, and I was an idiot kid who thought the girl of his dreams was finally choosing him. I wanted to talk to Benson first, but…did I mention I was seventeen? She came to me in lingerie, and I was a goner. So I did the unthinkable, certain they were over and I wasn't hurting anyone."

I lower the Daisy another inch.

"The next day, she went back to him, and I was wracked with guilt when he came to confide in me about how he was worried he almost lost her. I said nothing. And the next time they fought, I said nothing when she came to me. Or the next time. Or the next time. It wasn't until she pulled that stunt by claiming me as the father just to hurt Benson, that I realized she never cared about me at all. In fact, I was just a tool she used against him. Funny thing is, neither of us really loved her. We were just young and stupid, unaware that love isn't real unless it's reciprocated. We both just wanted the unobtainable."

I keep aiming the gun at him, but my finger is no longer on the trigger.

"She and Benson had been dating for a few months when Mom and John announced they were engaged. They'd only met because John insisted on meeting Sadie's boyfriend's parents. And since our Dad left us when we were younger, it was just Mom for him to meet. John's wife died when Sadie was two, and he'd been alone since then. Mom had been alone... In short, our family history got really complicated really fast."

"Benson said it was complicated," I mumble, looking down at the ground. "But that doesn't change the fact he didn't want me over there this week, and all along, the woman he gave a ring to was in his house, freshly divorced."

Yeah, I certainly didn't forget that tidbit that Benson shared. Talk about acid on an already burning wound.

"Sadie is the type of woman to never love a guy. She's always going to want them on the hook though. Benson and I are both older and wiser to her game nowadays. I can assure you that he never intended for anything at all to happen between them," he tells me.

I eye him like I'm suspicious of him, and he shrugs.

"Why'd he send you? Of all people?"

"No one else was brave enough to deal with your brothers, apparently."

I almost laugh. *Almost.*

"And I really want to make amends with my brother. It's been nine years. I miss him," he adds.

I couldn't imagine going nine years without my brothers. They'd kill someone if I was out of their lives for more than a few weeks. They had to visit me almost every other weekend when I was living in Seattle.

I think half the establishments there still have a poster of their faces to warn employees to *never* let them in again.

"What's your last name?" I ask.

"Calbert," he says reflexively, then slaps a hand over his mouth as though he didn't mean to say that.

I grin, knowing Benson must have told him not to tell me.

"Shit," he groans. "Don't tell him I told you. Does that mean you're considering forgiving him? Because really, this is all just one massive, slightly confusing, certainly understandable, misunderstanding."

I hear the sound of a Jeep pulling up behind my house, and a small smirk forms on my lips.

"I'll consider it. But he's probably going to have to work harder than this. I mean, it's not very manly to send his brother over because he's scared of my brothers."

He rolls his eyes.

"He's not scared of them; he just knew they'd make it impossible to speak to you. He knew they'd be keeping an eye on him. So he went into town, and then got your friend to draw them out. She's under the impression you're denying your feelings."

I don't tell him how much I already miss my best friend/boyfriend. His groveling game needs to be a little stronger than this if he really wants me back.

My smirk grows. "He's right. My brothers never would have left if he'd been right across the lake. But the problem now is that they just got back. And they're being really quiet. That's never good."

He looks around, seemingly unconcerned.

"I'm not really scared of two guys. I mean, I did see them wailing in pain after you finished with them."

It's positively adorable how clueless he is.

"No one has explained the four corners of the Wild Ones, have they?" I ask, amused.

He shakes his head slowly.

"The what?" he asks.

"First rule of family: brothers don't hit sisters. They take their beatings, because sisters only beat them when they deserve it."

I start backing up, closing the door in the process. "Good luck, Deacon. You're going to need it. You're about to learn what the Wild Ones really are."

He snorts, still unconcerned, and I listen for the first—

"Motherfucker!" I hear him roar, seconds before a series of loud pops ring out.

Then the whistle of a firework sounds as a scream pierces the air. I glance out the window to see Deacon running with his ass on fire, leaping into the lake on purpose as more fireworks shoot off in his direction.

I laugh to myself, knowing he deserves at least that much, even though I should probably thank him.

I guess Benson forgot to warn him my brother's don't always fight fair.

Eh. What the hell.

He'll survive.

Chapter **21**

Wild Ones Tip #100
Don't try to understand why we are the way we are.
You'll just get a headache and no answers.

BENSON

"Explain the Wild Ones to me," my brother says, hissing out a breath as he slides on a pair of pants.

I have to give it to him; he still wants to help me even after the brothers shot fireworks at him and lit his ass on fire with a homemade blow torch. He had to jump in that cold water to keep from getting seriously injured. As it is, it just left him with a little burn no worse than sunburn.

"At a metaphorical four corners of the lake, you have a different family representing a Wild family. Wild Ones are not allowed to date each other. They're not allowed to all be in one place at one time. At most, only two Wild One families can be in the same place at the same time. Never more. With the exception of certain circumstances."

His eyebrows are at his hairline.

"And this is normal to you?" he asks dubiously.

I smirk. "You grow used to it. The Vincents—Lilah included—are part of the Wild Ones. This is their corner. The Vincent brothers, as you've learned, can be ruthless. Usually they're harmless and only destructive to inanimate objects. Unless you piss them off."

"And the cops do nothing?"

"There's one cop. There're a lot of Wild Ones. Unless someone presses charges, there's no reason for police. And no one is stupid enough to press charges against anyone, because all the Wild Ones will come after you until they drive you out of town. The Vincents were the youngest addition. Lilah's father and mother made their name notorious, and the brothers and Lilah expanded on that."

He shakes his head, looking at me like I've lost my mind.

"You sound like you're proud of this."

My smile grows. "Lilah has both of them under her thumb, even though she likes to act like she doesn't. She knows, without a doubt, that if she told them to kill someone, they'd simply ask her where she wanted them to hide the body. So yeah, I'm proud to be with her, because she's tough but never acts like she runs this town. None of the Wild Ones do. They simply defend their own and mind their business, for the most part, when they're not bored and looking for a good time."

He groans as he shifts.

"Their *business* was burning my ass. I could have been seriously injured."

"If they thought you were too stupid to jump in the lake, they would have found another way to scare the shit out of you. They've tested all this stuff on each other—the brothers, not Lilah—before they use it on other people. It's 'fun' to them to test these things. They knew, down to the second, how long your ass could be on fire before it burned through your clothes or spread.

"That's just...insane."

I look out, seeing the flag flying high, taunting me. Lilah's at home. So close, yet so far away.

I bet her brothers are camouflaged and armed with pipe bombs right now. I have no choice but to take extreme measures.

"That's Tomahawk," I say, smiling tightly with a bittersweet taste in my mouth.

"And you've lived like this for nine years and we never knew when we came to visit," he says on a sigh.

"It only gets really crazy in the winters. During the summer, people seem to entertain themselves better. During the winter, the Wild Ones get restless."

He moves to the window, eyeing her flag as well.

"Does it make me a masochist that I want to see it in the winter now?" he asks seriously.

I'm not sure what's happening here, but I actually feel a little bit like I have a brother again. Not like before, but maybe one day.

I never thought that bridge could be repaired.

"That's Tomahawk. It draws you in with its craziness, and once you start rolling with it, you find it impossible to leave."

"Speaking of leaving, doesn't she know that's dangerous? To fly a flag when she's home and lower it when she's not? People always know her movements."

I snort, then double over and outright laugh.

"What?" he asks, confused.

"Her brothers set your ass on fire, and they knew you weren't a physical threat," I say around my laughter. "What the hell do you think would happen to an intruder?"

He pauses like he's thinking about it.

"If anyone ever tried to hurt one Wild One, all the Wild Ones would break the cardinal rule by coming together and joining forces, and hell would rain down on whatever idiot thought it was a good idea to break in or worse. And that's only if they survived the original Wild One. There's not a soul for a hundred miles who doesn't know this. It's why Tomahawk is the safest place to visit."

He massages his temples. "I feel like I've landed in another universe."

"No. Just a small lake town that literally has nothing much else to do but entertain itself. Born and raised in the wilderness makes you…different. Hell, living here for nine years has changed me."

He studies me for a moment. "I can tell. You seem to really be happy."

My eyes flick back to that damn flag.

"I will be happy. As soon as my water cannon gets here."

"Water cannon?" he asks, his voice going up an octave.

"There's only one way to win back the heart of a Wild One. You have to prove you're crazy enough to deserve it," I explain.

"But a water cannon? What the hell, man?"

"You still with me? I won't be able to execute the next part of my plan alone."

He sighs harshly. "Hell, might as well. Just tell me your next plan won't set my ass on fire."

"Nah. But just abandon ship if they manage to almost blow us up."

He pales as I walk over and grab my phone. I have some people to call.

"You're kidding, right?" he asks.

My eyes come up. "What part of Wild Ones don't you understand?"

Chapter 22

Wild Ones Tip #56
Chaos is not scary. It's sexy.

LILAH

"You love him," Aunt Penny says with no preamble.

She's the only one I've told the truth to since Benson hurt me three days ago.

"I can't love him. We've only been together for a little over two weeks," I point out, even though it sounds like a lame attempt at a protest.

I finish setting up her website, and turn it around for her to look at. She gushes over it for a second, then I turn it back around to fix her screen so she can check her orders easily.

She's officially selling her jams online.

"I was in love with Bill within a week of knowing him," she sighs wistfully. "It took him longer, but not by much. You and Benson...you two have been falling in love for years. You just didn't know it, because you never crossed that physical boundary until two weeks ago," she says, moving over to put some of her jams on the new shelves my uncle built her.

"We were friends. Not in love," I argue.

"How many days did you spend apart?" she muses.

I shrug, bristling a little.

"Not many."

"You two couldn't stop touching. Always leaning on each other, always laughing at your own inside jokes. And always, *always* seeking each other out first, no matter where you were."

I swallow the knot in my throat as I dare to peek up at her. Her eyes water when she sees the unshed tears in my eyes.

"I realize you've always been the rock. Your brothers always leaned on you. You saw how much it hurt them when you left them so you could go get some schooling for this career you chose. But you've let that hold you back from ever considering settling down, because you thought that meant you'd have to leave them, even though you don't. However, all along, Benson has been slowly taking over your heart. You just finally noticed it, kiddo. You've been in love for who knows how long. Having sex is just one small part of the relationship equation, and it has no effect on whether or not you're in love."

I try to shake my head again, but when that forces a tear to slip free, I freeze, worried I'll sling more loose.

As I wipe it away, she sits down in front of me. "You haven't been intimate with anyone in three years," she says quietly.

"Not a whole lot of options," I remind her.

She rolls her eyes. "I brought you all kinds of options from the lodge — very handsome men who were very interested. You never paid them any attention. Three years ago, something happened. You know what that is."

I do, but saying it aloud is almost like confirming what she's saying is true.

And if I'm in love with Benson, then my life is going to suck even more. Because it hurts to love someone you want to shoot a little.

And it's not like he's tried to get me back, other than sending his brother to me. Totally lame, by the way. And insulting. I'm a Vincent, and you send your brother to speak on your behalf?

"Say it," she tells me, peering at me expectantly.

I groan. "Benson and I became real friends three years ago."

Her smile spreads, even though it's watery. "And what cemented that friendship?"

"I couldn't get my boat to start, and he came over, tore it apart, spent the day working on it, even though it was cold. He finally just reassembled a new motor for me. After he was done, he went and threatened my brothers, told them to buy their own boat and never touch mine again, or they'd have to deal with him."

She rolls her eyes. "Only a Vincent would find that a bonding experience," she sighs. "And those wild brothers of yours respected him enough not to retaliate."

I can't help but smile, even as another tear trickles down my face.

"It was the first time someone else handled them, instead of cowering. I felt like I had some help to keep them in line. Also, I felt like I was no longer one-third. Killian and Hale have always been two-thirds together. Always together. Sometimes I think they share a brain."

To this, my aunt laughs loudly, nodding like she agrees.

"And sometimes I feel like I'm right there with them. But most of the time, I felt like I was the odd man out, always cleaning up after them, and constantly left out because I didn't always think like them. Then Benson...it's like we shared something. He was on my level, or at least cool with my level. And he had my back even when it came to my brothers."

I sigh, and she brushes a piece of hair behind my ear.

"That, my darling niece, is real love. It's not always going to slap you in the face, though that kind is amazing too. I would know. But sometimes, it burns you so subtly, that you don't realize you're boiling until it's too late. The water just took a while to heat up with you, kiddo."

She takes a breath like she's readying me for the grand finale.

"You've spent almost every day with him for three years. You've touched each other affectionately for three years. You've subconsciously sought each other out for three years. You've been in a steady burn for three long years. Now…the pot is boiling because you're finally ready."

"Except I'm not. He's over there with his ex-fiancée, the girl he planned a future with nine years ago, and I'm—"

A loud *boom* rattles the air, and my aunt and I both exchange horrified looks before darting to the door to see what my brothers have blown up.

The second we're outside, we freeze, staring as another *boom* rattles the air, and water sprays straight up. I cock my head, trying to figure out what's going on. But the scene before me makes no sense at all.

My breath catches in my throat when the water sprays up again, and I see the two boats racing toward each other.

"Please tell me they're not really throwing pipe bombs again," my aunt says dryly.

My brothers are in one boat. And two other brothers are in another—Benson and Deacon.

Benson cuts the wheel, and Deacon sprays water from a water cannon, blasting Hale as my brother readies to launch another pipe bomb. Hale is thrown from the boat when the water pummels him in the chest.

"Where'd he get a water cannon?" I ask on a breath.

"They're going to kill each other," Aunt Penny hisses, running down the stairs. "Our boys are supposed to be the damn Wild Ones. They're going to start a fifth corner if this shit keeps up."

Right. Right. A water cannon's origin is not the most important part of this right now.

I race after her as my uncle walks out of his shop, wiping his hands on a rag that's already stained with grease. His eyes widen when Killian gets blasted in the chest with the same water cannon.

Deacon howls with laughter when Killian finally falls off the side of the boat, killing the motor in the process. Deacon bumps fists with Benson as they circle my brothers like sharks.

"Where'd he get a water cannon?" Uncle Bill asks.

See? It's not just me. A freaking water cannon demands attention.

"Does he realize he's starting a war?" my aunt demands. "And what happens if they keep this up? The town will insist on a fifth corner. Who would move?"

The sound of cars pulling in behind us has me turning around, and I see people getting out of their vehicles, hurrying toward us. Tons of people too, not just a few.

"What the hell?" I ask on a long, confused breath.

"For once, I have no damn clue," Aunt Penny groans, looking over the ridiculous amount of uninvited guests.

Delaney is practically beaming as she races toward the edge to watch the showdown.

"If you want out, you have to promise on the graves not to throw another one of those fucking bombs. Ever," Benson tells them, moving over to take position behind the water cannon as Deacon takes over the boat's helm.

"Fuck. You," Hale seethes, starting to haul himself out.

Benson blasts him with the water cannon, and Hale flails backwards, slapping the water with a *clap* when he lands on his back.

"I must have heard you wrong," Benson says, grinning as he holds his finger on that trigger.

Seriously! Where'd he get a water cannon?

"Don't move to the wilderness, they said." Liam's voice has me jerking my head to the left to see him right beside me, his arms crossed over his chest as he stares out at the lake to see this bizarre turn of events.

"You'll be bored to death, they said," he goes on. "Peace and quiet gets old, they said." He turns and gives me an eye roll. "Funny how this wasn't in the town brochure."

I'd laugh under normal circumstances, but these are most definitely *not* normal circumstances.

"Wait…Tomahawk has a brochure?" I ask, unable to help myself.

"Yield or freeze to death. Your choice," Benson tells my brothers, reminding me there are far more important things going on than brochures.

"Damn it, they're going to freeze to death," I grumble.

"We'll yield the pipe bombs, but you still aren't getting near our sister," Killian acquiesces.

As if he's known exactly where I've been all along, Benson turns to face me, and he says something I can't hear to Deacon, as both my brothers start scrambling to get on their boat.

Benson's boat turns and shoots toward us, and he curses when Deacon doesn't line up correctly, bumping the dock too hard when he tries to dock it.

"Sorry. I don't drive a boat to the store in Seattle!" Deacon defends loudly.

Benson says something I can't hear, and hoists himself onto the dock before jogging my way.

I look for somewhere to hide, but there's really no way around this. Only problem is…I now notice half the town is here.

Benson doesn't stop until he's right in front of me, cupping the sides of my face.

My eyes stare into those dark brown ones, and he lets his gaze rake over me like he can't bear not seeing everything at once.

"I've been in love with you for over a year, Lilah Vincent. You're a different brand of crazy than I realized if you think I'm going to let you go now."

I almost fall forward when he releases me suddenly and takes a step back, smirking at me as he goes to stand on top of the picnic table. My heart is still pounding as I try to process the fact he just told me he loved me.

"I'm on the challenge committee, so I have the right to instate a new beard challenge if I want to," Benson says, drawing a few hushed whispers.

"There's a challenge committee?" Liam asks.

"And I will," Benson goes on, smirking over at me. "Unless Lilah Vincent tells me she's still mine, and that she's not ever going to leave me again."

I narrow my eyes when Delaney comes over and grips my arm painfully.

"Don't you dare let them grow back the beards," she hisses.

"The challenge was voted against once. It'll be voted against again," I point out, even though it's just a small act of defiance. He doesn't know it yet, but I'm already his. Never stopped being his.

And he won me over the second he took my brothers out with a freaking water cannon. Because I totally want to shoot them with it myself. I also really want to shoot the Malones. Maybe even the Nickels and Wilders too.

Aunt Penny is unfortunately right. I've loved the asshole for longer than I realized. And now I'm boiling.

Benson's eyes glint with determination as he stares me down.

"Unless the challenger assumes the punishment to instate the challenge on his own accord—don't forget that little clause. I'll swim to the other side of the lake. If I make it without being pulled out, the challenge is set. No one can refuse. It could be another nine years before it ends. What do you say, Lilah?"

He smirks, and I battle a grin.

"Really. I need some sort of rule book or something, and I want to be on this challenge committee," I hear Liam saying, and my uncle is quickly at his side, paperwork in hand.

"Seriously?" I ask my uncle and Liam as they start discussing the committee right beside me.

"Lilah, you're stalling," Benson says, sounding amused.

Sighing heavily, I stare at him, weighing my options. Say no, let the beards grow, walk around miserably missing my best friend, while the rest of the town hates me for the bad beards. Or say yes, have Benson back, let him spend an

obscene amount of time making all this up to me, and keep
the bad beards away.

Tough choice.

"I'll come back to you. On one condition," I say, crossing
my arms as I grin.

"What condition?" he asks, stepping off the picnic table,
but hesitating to move toward me again.

"Tell everyone here how you make your money." My lips
curl in delight, and he glares over at his brother.

Deacon groans while dropping his head back, knowing
I've Googled their name now and know their not-so-dirty
secret. There's a pun in there. You'll figure it out later.

Everyone perks up, completely interested in hearing if
he's going to cave to this demand. It would be a long-time
mystery finally solved. Only I have the answer right now. The
rest are salivating for a morsel.

"I'll just instate the challenge, and everyone here will be
pissed off at you," he argues, turning to go toward the lake
instead of coming to me.

Yeah…that deflates my bubble. About thirty angry
stares — men and women — swing my way as if cued.

"Lilah, so help me…" Delaney threatens, letting her voice
trail off. "Not even the Vincent name will keep us all at bay."

Cursing, I start chasing Benson, wondering if I should at
least let him jump in the water or not, when he suddenly spins
and grabs me like he knew I was close. He swallows my
sound of surprise when his lips crush mine, and he pulls me
to him as my eyes flutter shut.

It feels too good, too real, and too natural when his lips
are on mine, as though this is how it should have been all
along. My hands go up to the back of his neck, holding him in

place, and cheers erupt when he lifts me off the ground, kissing me thoroughly.

"Does this mean we can play with the water cannon now?" I hear Hale asking.

Benson breaks the kiss to glare at him. "Hell no."

I drag him back down to kiss me again, and catcalls follow it.

"The Wild One weddings are always the best," Aunt Penny says too happily behind me.

"Why?" I hear Liam asking, though it's just idle chitchat, because my attention is focused on the man who is walking me toward the dock.

"Because the Wild Ones can all come together for sanctioned events. When a Wild One gets married, it's the day of no rules. All the Wild Ones can join together for one, incredibly wild day."

More cheers erupt, and Benson grins against my lips. Aunt Penny isn't going to stop until we're married.

"Benson?" I say against his lips as he drops into the boat, pulling me onto his lap.

Deacon struggles with pushing away from the dock and starting the motor, but we let him figure it out. Learning experience and all.

"Yeah?" Benson answers, nibbling my bottom lip in a delicious way.

"You forgot to tell me you're a twin."

He breaks the kiss to pull back, studying me like he's confused. "So?"

"So? We're definitely never having kids. We'd end up with quintuplets or something."

His grin reforms, and his lips are back on mine. "I'm fine with that," he murmurs, stealing my sanity as the sound of boat motors rev in the background. "Because I want you all to myself for as long as I can have you."

"What the hell are they doing?" Deacon asks. He still hasn't gotten us started.

I look over to see my uncle and some of the other men on the boats, scooping out the fish that are floating to the top.

"They're making sure the fish don't go to waste," Benson answers before I can.

"Fish just float to the top?" Poor Deacon. He's so confused.

"Pipe bombs," I remind him.

"How have you hidden all this crazy from us for nine years?" Deacon asks his brother.

I arch my eyebrow as Benson smirks. "This is barely anything. You've only seen one corner of crazy," I point out. "We're the smallest corner too."

I can't tell if he looks terrified or intrigued. Maybe both.

"Fish fry tonight!" my uncle calls out, as my brothers shiver next to the fire my aunt has made.

Their clothes are in heaps on the shore, and they're wrapped in blankets. I wave at them, and they wave at me.

"See you tonight!" Hale calls out.

"Fish fry and we're invited," Killian adds.

My aunt just shakes her head like she's annoyed, but she smiles when her back is to them.

Benson's arms tighten around me as Deacon *finally* starts the boat. He's been paddling us way away from the dock. Yes. *Paddling* us. In a bass boat.

It's a good thing he doesn't live here. The guys would mock him mercilessly.

Deacon manages to make it across the lake — what feels like an hour later.

Benson gets up, depositing me to a seat in the back, and moves toward the front when Deacon gestures for him. Deacon still can't dock a boat — in case you've forgotten.

Benson pulls into his lift instead of tying off, and he presses the button that slowly cranks us up.

I climb out the second I can, and Deacon follows. Benson is the last out, but his hands are on me the second he's out, and his lips find mine.

I'm not sure how long we stand on that dock and kiss like we haven't seen each other in years, but I know I've forgotten everything by the time he finally breaks the kiss.

"Come on," he says on a sigh. "I want you to meet my family."

When I tense, he grips me tighter, making sure I can't run.

"I'm in love with *you*. I should have told you about Sadie being in our family, but I had no idea how to make that okay with our relationship so new."

I narrow my eyes. "I'm literally a Wild One. I could have handled it if I had been prepared, Benson. That's a fraction of the reason why I have to fly that damn flag in my yard when I'm home — because we can handle anything thrown at us. And to warn the neighbors I'm in — town rules and all that — but that's not the point. The point is that I can handle complicated and crazy. I just need to know you won't keep me in the dark when things are uncomfortable for you."

I'm looking up at him as he frowns down at me.

"You're right. And I'm sorry. But you kept on about not settling down for years, and then—"

I kiss him, dragging his head down to shut him up. He groans as he pulls me closer, and one of his hands goes to my hair, angling my face up even more. Finally, I smile against his lips.

"I didn't know how much fun settling down could be," I say against his lips, smiling.

He smiles back, and I start to tell him I love him…when I see his family is all on the deck and staring down at us. Sadie included.

I'd rather my first confession of love not be in front of his ex.

Benson looks over, and he takes a deep breath, his touch on me tensing.

His mother has tears in her eyes for some weird reason.

"So, do you guys want to go to a fish fry tonight?" I ask them.

Benson goes absolutely stiff, and Deacon grins at him.

"We'd love to!" his mother squeals. "Benson never lets us join him with townies."

I let it slide that she just called us townies.

"No one tells our last name," Benson says, pointing a finger at the little boy who looks over, confused.

"We're now the Nolans family," Deacon affirms.

"But why?" his dear, sweet mother asks so innocently.

"Because it's Tomahawk," I say with a smile, even as Benson's eyes narrow on me. "And in Tomahawk, there are four corners of crazy to represent the Wild Ones. They'd never leave him alone if they found out Benson—our beloved, bearded, awesome, *manly* Benson — was secretly the heir to a body wash empire."

A muscle jumps along Benson's jaw, but his eyes are smiling at me.

"What's wrong with body wash?" his stepfather asks.

I've always loved how Benson smells. And because I love him, I won't let the other Wild Ones know his secret. At least not until he's married to me and gains exemption that way.

"It's Tomahawk," Benson and I both say, only confusing everyone more.

"Unless your profession is as manly as they get, you keep your fucking mouth shut," Benson grumbles. "And I'm not an heir. I'm a shareholder in the family business that our mother started and turned into an empire. We're proud of her."

His mother beams, and I realize insulting the body wash empire would be devastatingly disrespectful.

"I love the way he smells," I say with a shrug. "But the other Wild Ones would never leave him be."

She nods determinedly, still rolling with the punches. I really like her.

"What's a Wild One?" Sadie asks, her eyes on me.

My lips curl into a dark grin. "We usually like blowing things up. Or hunting, because we're the best shots on the lake. Or fighting, because that's our favorite form of communication. Or we find something randomly dangerous to do when we're bored. In short, we're fucking crazy, sometimes dangerous, and worst…very unpredictable."

I wink at her, and she swallows hard.

Benson's arm slides around my waist, and he kisses the top of my head.

"I can't believe I never knew this town had so much excitement," Benson's mother says, her eyes alight with interest. "Let's go get changed for this fish fry," she adds, clapping her hands together, then she purses her lips. "What's a fish fry? And what does one wear to such a thing?"

I restrain a smile as Benson blows out a breath. He's going to catch hell for having a mother who worries about what to wear to a fish fry.

"Let's get in. I'll break it down for you," he tells her, still keeping me close.

"If it's all the same to you," Deacon starts, sidling up to Benson's other side, "I think I'm going to come back in a few months and stay for a while. This town has piqued my interest."

I look away, giving them the most privacy I can for this moment, since I'm pressed up against Benson's side and he's not letting me go.

I know the town isn't the reason Deacon wants to stay, and I know on some level, Benson just remembered how much fun it is to have a brother. Considering they went against *my* brothers.

And won!

And they didn't get blown up. Not that my brothers were actually trying to blow them up, but they were trying to blow enough water into the boat to rock their worlds.

They're better aims than that, and if they wanted to blow something up, they would.

"Make sure you're back before the end of fall," Benson says with a shrug. "Once the snow sets in and the lake freezes, it's hard to get out here. Impossible in that Mercedes you own. And if you're going to be sticking around, lose the Mercedes. Trust me. You'll never hear the end of it."

I look back just as Deacon smiles and directs his attention to the ground. "Sounds like a good idea."

His mother is watching them from the top when I look up, and she gives me a soft, somewhat appreciative smile that I don't understand.

Deacon jogs up the steps ahead of us, kissing his mother on the top of her head, before he walks in.

She speaks just as we step in front of her.

"Care if I have a word with Lilah in private?" she asks Benson.

He looks to me for permission, and I shrug. I have no idea what she wants to say to me, but...I figure she may be worried for her son's health. My brothers did just throw pipe bombs at him.

Somehow I don't think telling her they weren't actually trying to kill him will mean very much to her.

"I'll go get out of my wet clothes," Benson says, looking at me again. "Hurry up and join me."

I flash a grin, then remember his mother probably isn't used to such insinuations. I forget how normal people behave and all that.

She's blushing when I look back at her, and Benson walks off, leaving us to speak.

"Fish fries are very casual. If you have jeans, I'd wear them. And a T-shirt. Boots are the best for any event around here. Bugs are vicious," I say, babbling.

It occurs to me that I've never spoken to a guy's mother. At least not a guy I was getting *wild* with.

Her gaze drops to my combat boots, and she smiles as she looks back up to me.

"Thank you."

My eyebrows go up.

"No problem," I say with a shrug. "Never dress up, and you'll fit in around here anywhere you go."

Her smile broadens. "I meant, thank you for what you did for my sons. Benson doesn't even question your loyalty to him. He let his brother come see you. Alone. Because even though he'd hurt you, he knew without a doubt you'd never cross that line just to hurt him back. Because of you, my sons are speaking—actually speaking with smiles on their faces— for the first time in nine years."

She takes a deep breath as I try to figure out what to say.

"So thank you," she says again.

"Deacon was legit trying to mend things between them and never tried anything when he came to talk to me. And besides, Benson knows I'd have shot him if he had tried anything," I say casually, then realize, once again, that's not a response for a normal person.

She laughs under her breath.

"With a BB," I amend, as though that makes it all better.

She sighs long and hard. "I complicated their lives by marrying John. I never had a clue it could go so wrong for them. And Sadie…" She lets the words trail off as she looks back at me. "It took one girl to tear them apart, and it took one woman to bring them back together."

She touches my shoulder, gently clasping it.

"Now, do you have some boots I can borrow?" She eyes my waist, and I eye her very elegant trousers. "And some jeans?"

To this, I laugh.

"Let's steal Benson's boat. I have an entire wardrobe. Pants might be short, but the boots will cover that. But hurry. Because Benson hates it when I steal his boat."

Her grin spreads so wide that it has to hurt.

"We'll make one quick stop by the Malones. I owe them for the paintballs, and I really, *really* want to try out that water cannon," I add.

Her laughter pours out as she quickly follows me down the steps.

I have to help her onto the boat, then I start willing the lift to work quicker as it slowly lowers us into the water.

Just as I get the boat pushed away from the dock and rev the motor, Benson comes running out, his eyes wide and horrified when he sees his mother in the boat with me.

I turn up the radio, blowing him a kiss, as the telling music plays.

I mean…the song couldn't have better timing.

"I love you, Benson Nolans!" I shout, which only gives him one minute of pause where his smile breaks across his face.

"Gotta break it loose, gonna keep it movin' wild, gonna keep it swinging, baby, I'm a real wild child."

The smile fades quickly as reality sinks back in and the song playing finally registers. He starts yelling, panicking, as I laugh manically and gas it across the lake. My brothers hear the song playing and race toward the end of my aunt's dock as I swing it sideways, getting just close enough. Absently I hear the squeal from Benson's mom as we rock hard in the water from the harsh turn.

They're just in their boxers, grinning hugely as they race toward us. "You boys want to shoot a water cannon?" I call out.

"Hell yeah!" they shout.

They leap into the boat, and poor Benson's mother's eyes widen when she sees how they're dressed.

"Hi, Mrs. Benson's Mom," Hale and Killian both say, working their way around the boat as I gas it again.

Benson is still yelling at us from across the lake as I crank the volume up louder. My brothers howl into the air like wolves as we take the bend, moving faster up the lake.

I love this boat. It's so much faster than mine.

I glance back, seeing his mother smiling now as she relaxes, and I return my attention ahead. The song starts over, and I smile bigger, realizing *it really is* fate. The town only plays this song on repeat when they think the Wild Ones have been too quiet.

The beaver flag is flying high in the distance, letting me know we're about to get exactly what I want. Malones love their fishing days.

"Mount up, boys! Payback time!" I yell over the sound of the loud motor and whirring wind.

Hale and Killian both man the water cannon, sharing in this moment, as I round the last corner. The Malones are all out on their dock, predictably fishing, completely unaware of what's coming, until suddenly they're being blasted.

Kylie screeches, diving away from her fishing pole, laughing uncontrollably when she sees it's me. She takes cover as her cousins and father start falling into the lake, and I loop around, coming back as more Malones start racing toward the dock, fully armed with their trusty paintball guns.

I'm laughing with my brothers as they swivel the cannon and make another pass, blasting them before those weak little things can make it to us.

I look back at Benson's Mom, realizing not all the paintballs missed us as I drive like a hellion back toward our corner. There's a yellow splatter on her shoulder, and her eyes are wide as she gawks at me, her hair whipping wildly in the wind.

She's clutching her arm underneath where she took the hit. No doubt that'll bruise. But battle wounds just mean you've seen the real town. And raised a *little* hell.

"Welcome to Tomahawk!" I shout, pausing for my brothers to howl again. "Home of the Wild Ones!"

Epilogue

Wild Ones Tip #3
You can't tame a Wild One. You just have to go wild.

One week later…

LILAH

Benson's body moves over mine as he pulls my leg up, getting a better angle as my back arches off the bed. He drives into me over and over, and I claw at his shoulders, panting for air as he picks up the rhythm.

I'm moaning when we hear the loud sirens howling in the distance. Benson doesn't stop, and I try to ignore the sound.

He comes down on top of me, his mouth sealing over mine, and the swirl of his hips is what does it to me in the end. I cry out, breaking the kiss, and Benson follows right behind me, shuddering as he groans into the crook of my neck.

Still on a high, I hear the sirens wailing relentlessly.

"We have to go," I say, almost breathless.

"What? Why?"

"Sirens."

He curses as he pulls out of me, and I rush to the bathroom to clean up. He's already stabbing his legs into his pants when I come back out.

"I've heard those sirens a total of twenty times since I've lived here and never had to go to one of those meetings before," he grumbles, and I grin as I quickly dress, pulling my hair up too.

"You were never with one of the four corners before. Something tells me this is about you."

"Me?" he asks, his face paling as he hurriedly pulls on a shirt. "Why me?"

"It was your boat that hit the Malones last week."

"*You* stole the boat! With my mother onboard! Now, despite the fact she was bruised and slightly terrified, she can't wait to come back. She's coming two more times this year. We may even do Christmas here, for fuck's sake, if they can get someone to chopper them in."

His mom totally thinks I'm awesome. I'd fist bump myself if it wouldn't be weird.

My smile only grows, and he follows me down the stairs, both of us rushing toward the dock. I hop down to the boat first, taking the helm.

He lifts me out of the driver's seat—expectedly—and deposits me to the seat next to him as he cranks the boat and gasses us toward town. I stand and move behind him, wrapping my arms around his neck as my lips trail up the soft beard that he keeps tamed.

"I love you," I tell him, sounding all sweet and stuff.

"You're still not driving my boat ever again."

Yeah, he hides the keys these days.

"But you love me too," I remind him.

I feel his smile. "Yeah. I do." But as he parks the boat near one of the town docks, he turns to roll his eyes at me. "You're still not driving my boat."

I mock a pout, and he bends, kissing my lips as his fingers thread through my hair. The boat bumps the dock, reminding us to tie off.

We each tie off an end, and I haul myself onto the shorter dock with ease. Ours have to be higher than the town limits, because of flooding issues.

Our fingers lace together as we walk toward the town hall where the skull-and-crossbones flag is flying high, something you rarely ever see unless there's an emergency.

Just as we walk in, Benson's breath rushes out. He looks around as if in awe.

"What?" I ask, tugging him toward our section.

His feet hesitate before he finally starts moving, his eyes still shifting around the room.

"I've never seen so many in one place before."

I laugh under my breath. "Because the Wild Ones aren't allowed to be together in one place unless there are special circumstances or sanctioned events. But when those sirens sound and that flag flies…you don't resist the call of the wild."

I wink, and he rolls his eyes, getting over his momentary awe state as we take a seat in my section.

Vick, our poor, lone officer, stands behind the podium, banging the gavel to get our attention.

"I'll keep this brief," he says as my brothers quickly join us, sitting down beside me, "since you all can't be together too long without mayhem quickly following. The troopers are coming into town in a few weeks."

Everyone groans, and he bangs the gavel again.

"We know this happens every summer. You get too rowdy, vacationers cause a fuss, and before you know it, the troopers drop in. It's rarely ever the same ones twice, because, let's face it, you run them off real good. But remember the rules: don't be seen, and don't get caught doing anything illegal. Make them go away without alerting them to the way our town works. Otherwise, we'll never get rid of them, and no one wants that."

He clears his throat. Considering he's the local pot distributor, he's always worried about trooper season.

Don't judge. You know by now we aren't conventional.

None of the locals like troopers. It interferes with our not-always-lawful way of life. In Tomahawk, you make money the best way you can. We do things a little under the government's radar. Nothing harder than pot allowed in town. Business licenses are iffy at best. And you might find a few unlicensed moonshine distilleries up and down the lake too.

Though it's legal to have pot in Washington…I'm almost positive it's not legal to grow it. And we don't exactly have dispensaries where taxes get a big cut. We have Vick.

Troopers make life hard for about a week. Two weeks has been the record.

"Who wants to start the pool?" Eric Malone asks.

"Two days!" someone shouts.

"One week," I say, waving a ten in the air.

"You can arrange the pool via internet. Not in here," Vick interrupts, and I lower my ten as Benson grins.

"Now onto the matter of the Vincents."

His eyes cut toward us, and Benson stiffens.

Hale stands, smoothing his hair back as he flashes a smile at us. His gaze returns to Vick.

"You sure you want to do this?" Vick asks.

"He does have a water cannon," Killian says as he stands next to Hale.

Benson goes stiffer, and I bounce in my seat with excitement.

"Benson Nolans," Vick starts, looking around at everyone else, "has apparently gone wild."

Wolf howls erupt around the room, and Benson mutters a curse under his breath. He's now officially among the Wild Ones, which means he'll be getting hit with paintballs, and various other things.

"Instead of building a fifth corner amendment, he's joining the Vincents, since he and Lilah will be getting married."

Hey!

"We actually haven't decided on that yet," I interject.

"You'll be getting married," Vick says dismissively.

"That's going to make their side bigger," someone points out—I think it's Lenny Nickel.

"We're the smallest corner," Hale says dismissively.

"Because we're the youngest addition," Killian adds, "we have room to grow."

"But the Vincents sprout in multiples," Kylie Malone says, winking over at me as I roll my eyes.

She knows I fear this.

"God help us all when they procreate," someone in the back says—not a Wild One.

"It's already done. Benson will become a Vincent when he marries Lilah—"

"I'm sorry, but *what*?" Benson asks, his eyebrows going up as I giggle to myself.

"You'll become a Vincent," Vick repeats. "You'll have to change your name. You know we can't have other names in the four corners. It'll confuse things."

"We're simple people," I drawl, grinning as Benson narrows his eyes down at me.

"Benson will become a Vincent, and be an addition to the dead chipmunk corner," Vick declares with finality.

"Apparently I don't get a say in this," Benson mutters.

"Just remember you love Tomahawk because of all the crazy," I say, patting his hand.

He tosses his arm around me as I lean into his side.

Vick points his gavel at Benson. "Install a flag immediately. You're officially a Wild One."

And that's our story.

We're a crazy, somewhat bizarre, certainly wacky town that makes life work and lives it to the fullest.

We're fierce.

We're loyal.

We're occasionally destructive.

We're undoubtedly wild.

Because we're the Wild Ones.

And we're just getting started.

The end.

For a sneak peek at Liam and Kylie's book, keep reading.

GOING WILD

The Wild Ones #2

Coming soon…

PROLOGUE

LIAM

People often ask me what in the hell convinced me to move to Tomahawk, Washington, where the four corners of crazy are known as the Wild Ones. They want to know what possessed me to live next door to the Vincents — the same ones who think it's acceptable to fish with dynamite if the fish aren't biting the hooks they so generously attempt to use.

They want to know why I ever thought I'd make it in the woods with bugs, bears, and other things that want to take a bite out of me.

I tell them all the same thing…it's a long, crazy story.

And of course, I blame one girl.

Chapter 1

Wild Ones Tip #293
Watch for Wild Ones. Shit usually blows up in our wake.

KYLIE

"You crazy sons of bitches!" I yell as the smoke slightly clears from where Hale Vincent has just *accidentally* blown up our dock.

His eyes are wide as he heaves himself out of the lake, his terribly long beard dripping with water.

"That was an accident!" he calls out. "I was aiming for the stump and tripped!"

Killian, his brother, points to the said stump that is lifting out of the water.

"It messed up our props the other day!" Killian tries to explain.

A grin spreads over my face when I hear the stampede of feet rushing this way.

"Better run, Vincents," I say with small smile.

Killian curses, trying to crank the boat, but he's too late.

Paintballs start flying, pelting the boys as they yelp and try to duck. The *tink tink tink* is a beautiful sound as the paintballs rapidly crash against the boat, while the army of Malones face off against two-thirds of the Vincent triplets.

"We'll fix it!" Hale yells as Killian gasses the boat and drives them away from the dock...or what's left of it.

"Damn right they'll fucking fix it," my dad grumbles, walking over as part of the dock breaks off and falls into the water, punctuating the destructive wake of the Vincents.

He groans.

"Damn Vincents. If I hadn't loved their Momma and Daddy so much, I'd kick their asses all day every day for the rest of my life."

I grin, knowing he's full of shit. He has a soft spot for the orphaned triplets. Just like the whole town does.

"It's not like we're much better," Eric points out helpfully.

"We're all the Wild Ones for a reason," Jason, another cousin of mine, says, grinning. "Besides, this means we can pay them back."

Dad points his finger in Jason's face. "Do *not* blow up their dock. Bill will never let me hear the end of it. Besides, Vick said he was going to put a ban on explosives if we all kept using them so much."

Tomahawk problems. Gotta love them.

"You sure you want to go off to LA and miss all this?" Dad asks, his beard moving up, signaling the fact he's smiling.

Or so I assume.

Tomahawk—land of the bushy beards. Don't ask. Long story.

Those beards are the reason I love traveling. I don't even know what the men from this town look like, so if I want my vagina to ever get any exercise…I travel.

For good reason.

Besides, most of the guys here are too afraid to hook up with a Wild One.

Pansies.

"It's just for a couple of months," I remind him.

He smiles broader, because that beard lifts higher.

"My fancy artist daughter."

I roll my eyes, and my cousins start heckling me. When Heath's muddy foot brushes my boot, my body turns to stone, and I slowly look down.

A hushed silence falls over the yard.

No one moves. Even the creatures of the forest seem to freeze in place, terrified of what I may or may not do.

My red. Beautiful. Shiny. Awesome Boots.

Mud.

Dirty. Mucky. Mud.

"Oh shit," Heath says on a hiss.

Slowly, my eyes come back up, leveling him with a cold glare. His eyes widen in fear seconds before he takes off running.

I snatch up the paintball gun, and I take aim before firing rapidly, hitting him at least ten times before he collapses and curls into the fetal position.

"You better be glad mud will wash off these!" I yell. Then peg his ass five more times with paintballs as he howls in pain.

My dad is shaking with silent laughter when I glare over at him.

"Just mud. You don't kill over mud if it's not the suede." He raises his hands innocently, and I roll my eyes.

"I'm going to go see Lilah before I leave. So I guess I need a ride there."

"I'm not going around the Vincents," he growls. "Not after they just blew up my dock."

I bat an unconcerned hand. "They'll fix it. They always do. It's only Lilah's shit they never fully repair."

"Take the boat. I'll send Heath after it."

I give him a quick kiss on his hairy cheek, and then he kisses my forehead.

"Be careful in LA. Don't get arrested. They're not as lenient as we are around here."

I flash a grin. "No worries. I won't be beating boys up on the sidewalks or accidentally blowing up someone's personal property."

"I mean it, Kylie. Don't do anything crazy like crashing your car into a pool again. You'll have to pretend to be normal for a couple of months and forget your raising. We won't be there to back you up," he goes on.

"I won't be crazy anywhere but Tomahawk," I tell him, crossing my heart with my index finger.

"Promise?" he asks.

"Promise."

Chapter 2

Wild Ones Tip #74
Wild Ones are always wild, so lock your doors and sleep in body armor.

KYLIE

"Hey, everyone, this is Kylie Malone, and she's filling in for Jake's pussy ass tomorrow so we have that fifth," Rudy says as we drop to a booth inside a bar.

It's a laidback bar, just on the outskirts of LA, not far from where the gallery was.

I flash a smile at all the guys around the table, my gaze lingering on one seriously sexy face for a moment longer than the rest, before giving a little wave.

The sexy guy arches an unimpressed eyebrow at me as he lowers his beer bottle.

He's blond, the perfect splash of tan, and has a strong jaw with no hint of stubble. I've been stuck in beard central for the vast majority of my adult life, so I'm still adjusting to the smooth faces.

And his is my favorite so far.

"You're going skydiving with us?" Sexy Guy asks skeptically, and I restrain a secretive smile.

"Yeah. Problem with that?"

He shakes his head slowly, his smirk lazily etching up. I can tell he's going to be a dick.

"That's Liam," Rudy says, gesturing to the dick.

He goes around the table, introducing the other three guys, and I pretend I don't feel the disbelieving gaze of Liam as he studies me without subtlety.

As I'm about to tell one of them where I'm from, Liam talks over us.

"This is expert level skydiving. No instructors are going to be strapped to you."

Guys like this? Never get challenged. I've learned that about LA in the past three weeks. I'm only here for four more, which will be the end of my showcase tour.

So far, I've learned it's nothing like what I'm used to.

But I'm also nothing like they're used to.

"Really? I had no idea." I mock a gasp. "Rudy, why didn't you tell me?"

Really, though, my acting skills are so over-the-top that you can hear the sarcasm coating each word. Rudy starts laughing, and Liam's cocky smirk flattens to a thin, disapproving line. I wink at him before ordering a shot of tequila.

"Shots? Before skydiving?" Liam asks.

"You always mother the ones around you?" I ask absently, not looking directly at him.

Really is a shame such a sexy face belongs to such a prick.

Five minutes into speaking to him, I know three things.

He's entitled.

He's rich.

He's a prick.

All I need to know.

My shot arrives, and I grin up at the waitress, thanking her before handing her my money. Then I toss it back and order another.

She keeps them coming, and before I know it, the conversation has veered to the more pornographic pieces that were in the gallery today. I laugh under my breath, trying not to notice how Liam is still studying me.

"You always have such curly hair?" he asks as I stack up my fifth empty shot glass.

"You always stare at curly hair? Or am I just special?" I ask, tugging a light brown curl of mine that springs back into place when I let go.

I smirk at him this time. It seems to bother him when I don't let him bother me.

He spins the coaster on the table, not looking at me anymore, and I go back to pretending to listen to the conversation.

I mean, Rudy offered me a free spot on their dive, and usually, a dive like this would run close to seven hundred dollars, possibly more. I couldn't pass it up, so I can pretend to like them for a night.

Even Liam.

The prick.

The guy who is staring at me again.

My hair is shoulder length, and I swear, I have those ringlet curls that turn to straight fuzz if I don't use a thousand hair products.

There's something you should know about where I come from…

The women may dress like something out of a fashion horror magazine, but we damn well take care of our hair.

Long story for another time.

I stand and move toward the jukebox when the weight of his very scrutinizing gaze continues to follow me. I pick a song I love, mostly to remind me of who I am, and walk back when it starts playing.

Liam's eyes slowly scan down the front of my little white sundress and drop to my boots—okay, this is where I tell you I have a small issue. Well, it's a big issue. An obsession, really.

Cowboy boots.

My small apartment back home has two walls full of boots.

No lie.

It's where most of my money goes.

Don't judge me. It's an addiction.

"Nice boots," he says, his lips twitching as I sit down. "Straight off the ranch?"

Oh, this guy is really close to getting his ass kicked by these boots.

"I'm a real wild child," catches my attention as someone from the bar sings along.

My grin spreads, and I turn back to face the prick. "These boots are made for walking," I joke as I stand again, move to the dance floor, and dance with the first guy who has the balls to join me.

I have no idea what his name is, but he's a sweetheart, and a damn good dancer.

I'm laughing and enjoying myself, when I turn and see Liam watching me, like he's trying to figure me out. I go back to ignoring him as someone else starts playing the song over.

It makes me a little homesick, but it gives me a piece of home at the same time.

I keep taking shots. And I keep dancing, enjoying myself.

Several other songs play, and before I know it, the once-empty dance floor is now packed full of people. I dance until I'm suddenly plowing against a firm body, and I move a curl out of my face to look up at…Liam.

He smirks down at me.

"How is it you've now had ten shots, yet you still seem mostly sober?" he asks, handing me yet another shot of tequila.

"I'm very sober. Are you counting my shots?" I ask, shooting the drink without thinking about the fact he might have done something to it.

I'm not used to having to be wary.

If I feel funny in a second, I'm going to karate chop his dick so hard, he'll never be able to get it up again.

He smirks before mouthing, *"Eleven."*

And then he winks at me.

Even though I hate him a little, and wonder if he's poisoned or drugged me, for some reason I still smile. His eyes dart down to my lips, and then they flick back up to meet my eyes. He seems amused more than anything.

"Are you going to answer my question?"

I roll my eyes, still dancing. "Two reasons. One, my family are big drinkers. You grow a tolerance, because no one wants to be the first one who's drunk at a family event. Two, the shot glasses are half the size of normal shot glasses. And they only fill them half way up. So I've maybe had three shots in reality."

He cocks his head like he's studying me.

"And you're just dancing because…"

My eyebrows go up. "I *like* dancing. Besides, if I had stayed over there, something terrible would have happened."

He waits expectantly, and I grin at him.

"What?" he finally asks, taking the bait.

"You would have just kept smirking at me and delivering veiled insults."

His smile spreads for the first time. A real, genuine smile.

I'm human, and I'm capable and crass enough to admit that smile of his is like a live wire straight to my clit. Not that I'd ever tell him that.

"That would be terrible, I suppose," he says, stepping closer.

"Very," I agree, wondering if I'm crossing into flirty territory when he tucks another curl behind my ear.

I might even shiver a little when his fingers brush my cheek during the motion. This guy smells as good as he looks. And it's been…six months? At least six months since the last time I found someone to scratch an itch with.

"You really sure you can skydive? Because tomorrow is no joke," he says seriously.

My lips twitch.

"You skydive often?" I ask, vaguely aware we're just standing in the middle of a bunch of people dancing.

"Not too often anymore, but still on occasion. I like the rush it gives me."

"I'm well-acquainted with adrenaline rushes," I say with a shrug.

He gives me a dubious look that tells me he doesn't believe me, but I hold my secretive smile in place, not elaborating.

"You're a confusing little specimen, Kylie Malone," he says. I'm not sure why my name sounds so good coming off his lips.

I blame it on all the beards I've endured for too long. Our town stopped fornicating when the beards got long enough to hide baby birds in them. The whole nest and momma bird too, in some cases.

"I'm actually simple. We all are." I smile again.

"Simple? We? Who's we?" he muses.

"My family. Friends. Everyone back home."

"On the ranch?" he asks, but this time his tone is light and teasing instead of insulting.

"Back at the lake. No ranching."

"They wear cowboy boots on the lake?"

"I wear them."

He tugs one of my curls, and I allow him to keep invading my space. His foot is touching mine, but it's not offending my boot yet. If he scuffs a boot, I really will kick his ass. Then kick it some more.

"What were you showcasing at the gallery?" he asks, not bothered by the bodies bumping into us as they dance around our unmoving ones.

"Several pieces, actually. Why? Did you come peruse the massive showing?"

He cocks his head, his own secretive smile etching up. "I own the gallery."

Well, damn.

My eyebrows go up, and he smiles cockier. He's proud of his money and prestige, I guess.

I grab the sides of his face, and his smile dies as I tug his face down. He acts like he's about to struggle when I narrow my eyes and make a show of looking him over.

"Funny. I was thinking you to be more of the model type. Perfect symmetry."

His eyebrows go up again, and he stares at me like he thinks I'm crazy, while I keep his face smashed between my hands, giving his lips a bit of a fish pucker effect.

"You truly are a beautiful man," I say on a long sigh as I release the sides of his face.

"Beautiful?" he asks, laughing lightly.

"Yes. A beautiful...prick."

I pat the side of his cheek, and all the humor in his expression disappears.

"See you tomorrow, Pretty Boy," I say over my shoulder as I sashay away in my *awesome* boots. "See you guys bright and early," I say cheerily to the table of artists.

"You okay to walk back to your place alone?" Rudy asks so helpfully.

I wink at him. "Don't worry. I'll give someone hell if they fuck with me."

I grab my purse, and Liam is suddenly back at the table.

"Someone should walk you back to your hotel," Liam says firmly.

My smile creeps up, and I peer over at him. "I'm not at a hotel. I'm staying with a family friend. And don't worry," I tell him as I walk away. Without turning around, I loudly add, "I'm a Wild One."

Note from the author:

Thank you so much for reading the first book of the Wild Ones. This was a side project I wanted to do because I needed something light and fun to break up the more serious or darker books I'd been writing.

My heart needed a break.

Even my romantic comedies have some heavy subject matters at times. I just wanted something carefree, maybe even a little silly, with low intensity so you don't have your stomach in knots, your heart ripped out, or your soul stained for all eternity or whatever. ;) Nothing too deep or heavy.

With so many intense reads, sometimes you just need a fun book to reset yourself and break them up. I needed to write this to refresh myself, and this is my fun, simple, somewhat crazy series that makes me smile.

I really hope it makes you smile too, because there are several more Wild Ones to come, if all goes according to plan.

Kylie Malone's story is next, since *Becoming A Vincent* leads you into that with Liam's tale of why he moved to Tomahawk, land of the beardless ex beards. (Don't worry. Most still have beards, but they're just kept neat instead of collecting trays of food now.) It'll start in the past to show you how they initially met, then fast forward to the present where they finally meet again.

After hers, the plan (which could change, based on how the writing process goes) is to release Kai Wilder. Finally getting some of those Wild Men.

Anyway, thank you for giving this one a chance, even if it wasn't for you. I'd love to see your reviews, and they always help a book get noticed by others the more reviews an author collects — good or bad.

Now, to tell you just a little about the Wild Ones — a lot of the crazy came from my real life. I wanted wilderness, funny, crazy, outrageous, little civilization, and a very small /backwoods town. Welcome to Tomahawk. ;)

Nothing about this series is going to be mature. This is completely wild and outlandish, which is its intent.

By now, if you've followed me, you realize I'm not exactly normal.

Though we're a family of bullshitters and fish tales, we also had tons of real stories to share with people that no one ever believed…until they saw it. And then they either loved us or hated us.

My father liked to shoot a Coke can (never Pepsi) out of my uncle's hand just to prove he was a good shot, and my uncle always went along. He still has both hands. They got dynamite one time — fish really do float to the top if they were near (but not actually inside) the blast, or at least they did that week.

Don't worry — the fish got eaten and there wasn't *that* many since this was a pond and not a lake. ;)

We got a really dirt cheap four-wheeler (yes, I realize not everyone calls them this), and the plastic upper frame was held to the actual mechanical part (how's that awesome terminology for you?) with bungie cords. No joke.

I crashed it into the deep end of the pond, had to use a backhoe and logging chain to get it out, and pretend I had no idea why it was tore up when my dad got home.

Half of my dad's backyard is full of buried broken things, since we couldn't hide broken shit in the trash. He always carried the trash to work because he was too cheap for trash service—this is still a funny point of conversation with my family. Anyway, if you broke something, you buried it, because we had so many knickknacks that no one noticed something missing. Fortunately.

Unless it was a really expensive dolphin figurine…that always sucked. Prepare to do the grossest shit imaginable—clean porta potties type of gross—in order to pay back the money for a damn expensive glass dolphin. Punishments could be creative when my dad was in a funny-guy mood.

I'm getting off track.

That's just one tip of the iceberg there. I'll share a little more with you as the series goes on, if you want. I'll also be using a lot of that in these books.

Bottom line, what you may find crazy might have been something I pulled from my actual life. Or an exaggerated version of it. Hopefully that makes it a little more fun to read when you're guessing if it really happened or not. And the books, of course, will only get crazier.

(I like to ease people into the madness so they don't see just how deep they've gotten until it's too late and they realize they're a little crazy too.)

I have some of the absolute best memories from my semi-reckless childhood because of all the crazy ways we found to not be bored—days before internet was a household commonality; before the smart phone gave you unlimited entertainment at your fingertips (which means you had to be creative or stay hella bored); and before social media could forever document the photos of stupid things you'd probably like no one else to ever know about.

(Thank fuck social media happened AFTER I had a child and not before…)

As always, I appreciate each and everyone's support. You have no idea how much it means to me to bring these stories to life and have an incredible set of readers who support me.

Time to stop writing to you before I get teary-eyed for the first time in the book.

Btw, I love the hell out of you.

—CM

About the Author:

C.M. Owens is a *USA Today* Bestselling author of over 30 novels. She always loves a good laugh, and lives and breathes the emotions of the characters she becomes attached to. Though she came from a family of musicians, she has zero abilities with instruments, sounds like a strangled cat when she sings, and her dancing is downright embarrassing. Just ask anyone who knows her. Her creativity rests solely in the written word. Her family is grateful that she gave up her quest to become a famous singer.

You can find her on Facebook, Twitter, and Instagram.

Instagram: @cmowensauthor

Twitter: @cmowensauthor

Facebook: @CMOwensAuthor

There are two Facebook groups, the teaser group, and the book club where you can always find her hanging out with her fans and readers.

www.cmowensbooks.com

Sign up for my newsletter and get no more than one email a month with new release information and/or a list of my fave books from other authors and deals. (No spamming from me and no one else will get your email address from me.)

Printed in Great Britain
by Amazon

68853546R00124